EMILY COLLINS

Promises of August

a novel

Prologue

Dear Elena,

I'm sorry I haven't been writing recently. Grandpa wasn't doing too well for a while, and honestly, neither was I. He was my best friend, aside from you, really, and now he's gone. It's just hard to accept that sometimes and move forward with everyday life, especially with the way this has taken a toll on Mom. She's really excited to see you this summer. I think we could all use a change of scenery and the peace that is the ocean and that perfect salty air. I hope you know that my not writing has nothing to do with you and everything to do with me just trying to deal. I've been pouring myself into my music recently. I hope you'll give some of the lyrics a read when you come. I need another writer's eye, haha. I hope you've still been writing and that you still feel comfortable sharing it with me. I've read every single letter you've written and appreciated them all. I just couldn't bring myself to put pen to paper and write how I was feeling. I didn't even really know how I was feeling. I was numb. I guess you could say I had been experiencing the ultimate writer's block when it came to writing back. I am so sorry I missed your birthday, and I hope you won't kill me for saying that I honestly forgot and didn't even realize we had shifted into the month of November until Mom told me, and then I was too ashamed to even write. I've been in such a rut for so long, El. There's so much I have to tell you, and I hope we can pick up right where we left off two summers ago. I want to boogie board all day until I've swallowed up more salt water than I can take. I want to bike to the Library Cafe and have our writing sessions. And, I want my mom to catch a break and talk about the books she's reading with you and Nana.

She needs an escape this summer. We both do. I need our perfect beach town life to remind me that there are always beautiful things to appreciate in life. I need an escape from reality. Again, I am sorry for being so flaky, but you won't be able to get rid of me this summer, I can promise you that. I promise I will never go this long without writing again. See you soon, El.

- Henry

Oh! P.S. I am bringing my cousin Jason with me this summer. He's been visiting with us just to be here in the midst of everything. He's great, around your sister's age. Okay, that's all. Please don't kill me for not writing when you see me.

1

Chapter One

***

I read the letter over again a third time as we make our way to Cracker Barrel for our first stop on the trip. I have been dreaming of the Old Timer's breakfast meal since Clara basically pulled me out of bed this morning before the sun had even risen. On any normal early morning, I would have yelled at her to get out and fallen back asleep for another hour or two, but today is the only exception. When it finally comes time to make our way to my favorite escape every summer. Each time August has rolled around since my little sister, Clara, was born, I have gone to the same small town, filled with salty air, ice cream shops, and Alvin's Island Souvenirs on every corner, where condos line the deepest blue ocean for miles and miles.

There are pictures of oranges on every T-shirt as it reads, "Orange Beach. Small Town, Big Beach." After a couple years of going every summer, my mom took it as her opportunity for a break herself, from us "kids" that is, and that's when it became our annual tradition with just my little sister, grandparents, and I. Around our third summer there, a family started staying in the beach house next door that had always been vacant for as long as I had known. That's when I met Henry. At first, I was annoyed because suddenly there was a boy using "my ocean," as I called it, but eventually, as his family came each year, I learned to share our part of the sand.

His mom, Jules, and my Nana would sit together and listen to the waves for hours as they read their romance books that more than likely took place on North Carolina beaches. Meanwhile, my Papa and Henry's Grandpa Joe would sit under the umbrella talking about fishing, golf, or the stock market. Clara would always stay in a rotation of swimming in the pool and making new friends to build sand castles with, as the simplicity of being young and able to make friends in a matter of minutes had not yet been robbed from her. Henry had to grow on me, but after a few August's filled with him having cannonball competitions with me, looking for perfect sea shells together, and one in particular where he pushed another boy into the pool, fully clothed might I add, for making fun of me when I had my first ever swimsuit malfunction, he became my best friend.

He's two years older than I, but he's always said that he feels as if I'm older than he is. An "old-soul" he calls me, or "old-lady" when he's annoyed with my wanting to go to bed early and come in from late-night crab hunting that never results in us actually catching any. He has been my best friend for over half my life, constantly communicating through letters as we both discovered our passion for writing when we were in middle school and realized it was odd for both of us to get excited about writing papers. From Colorado to South Carolina, we would write to each other through every school year, and even through college until we finally made it to August, and we got to live our favorite five weeks of the year together in our favorite place. There was never a month when we didn't write to each other, until now.

The letter I currently hold in my hands is the first from him in just over nine months. Nine months. I only heard from him a couple of times after his grandpa Joe passed away late last July. My family and I went to the funeral, and I could tell that it was going to take him a while to be himself again. That was the first August his family didn't come to Orange Beach. It didn't feel the same without his family, especially knowing Grandpa Joe would never return. He started the whole tradition of every August together when he brought Henry's family.

I sent Henry letter after letter from the end of August on, and even tried calling, though we never would normally do that. Written words were one of our special ways of communication. That and the ability to just read each other with one look, though we only ever experienced that when we were together at the beach. I haven't gotten to experience that in nearly a year now. The last look we exchanged was a heartbroken one at Grandpa Joe's funeral. Regardless of the lack of seeing him, writing was something I thought we'd always have... until I wrote that last letter back in November.

I had written it after my birthday had come and gone, and I heard nothing from him. I was so torn about what to do. I knew he was hurting, but in his hurt, he also hurt me. Hurt people really do hurt people, I guess. I've been so stuck in between a place of complete understanding and confusion when it comes to our friendship recently, and how I've been feeling. I wrote him one last letter after my birthday had passed, telling him that I missed him, but I would no longer waste any ink on trying to reach out to him until he was ready. Since that last letter to him, I've quit my unfulfilling job to move back in with my parents, and all of my friends moved away to start the next phase of their lives. I've never really done well being alone, and now I spend more time with myself than anyone else. On top of this, I, too, have been mourning his Grandpa, whom I liked to call my "bonus grandpa."

All of these things, Henry has no idea about. My sister Clara and I have gotten so much closer, and so it's been nice to have time together before she leaves for college. But, then what do I do when she leaves? I don't know why, but I feel nervous about this summer. Distance has changed things, and I'm wondering if Henry and I can return to normalcy after so long. He's missed so much. He doesn't know anything about my life right now, and so much has changed. And, I definitely feel that I have too. I am two years post-grad, unemployed, and an aspiring writer. I have no idea what's next for me. But, no matter what has or hasn't happened, the tradition still remains.

My sister currently rides next to me, headphones in and face plopped against a pillow on the armrest as she is out cold with messy hair that she didn't bother brushing before we left. *The Beatles Radio* is playing from the front while Papa's eyes are hidden behind his sunglasses, one hand on the wheel as he whistles along. Nana clutches her favorite Nicholas Sparks novel while her freshly red-painted nails turn the pages, eager to keep reading. I look out the window as the trees pass, AirPods in, listening to songs that make me feel like my life is a movie… headed to the one place where you could convince me for a short time… that it actually is.

Chapter Two

***

We finally get off the interstate and pull onto that all too familiar highway that ends at the ocean. Clara slept almost the entire way while I just stared out the window in anticipation of what this August would bring. We pass mine and Henry's favorite spot, the Library Cafe, and I look at the letter stuffed in my bag again. I don't know how I will react when I see him, or what I will say, but I still have a day to prepare myself. Henry and his family won't arrive until later tomorrow night, and I fully plan on hogging the beach until then. I'm going to enjoy "my ocean" and escape into the words of Emily Henry that will surely distract me from my problems and immerse me in the perfect beach read.

We are about fifteen minutes away from the house now, and Clara and I are already gathering our things together as Nana asks us what we want from the grocery store. "Pineapple!" We both scream in unison. There's just something different about fruit at the beach, and every year I swear we go through like ten pineapples in the entire month of August.

As we pull into the driveway, I immediately feel the tension release from my shoulders while looking at the quaint, two-story, rustic white house. We pull under the side of the house, parking directly beneath the first floor, as the house sits on stilts. *Finally, hello, perfect beach escape. Hello August.* Nana gets out and switches to the driver's seat, ready to start the first tradition of the summer. Upon every arrival, without fail, she goes to get the groceries without any distractions, and Clara and I run up to the house to immediately claim our beds before rushing to the ocean. Of course, Clara wants the bed closest to the window with a view of the ocean.

"I call this side!" She says as she immediately throws her purse and blanket from the drive onto the bed to mark her territory. I just laugh in response.

When we were younger, we would always argue and shout. "*You had it last time!" No, you did!*" Now, I just let her have it. I could sleep on the front porch swing, wrapped up in the pastel blankets and pillows that cover it, and overlook the ocean every night for all I care. All I've wanted all year is to be back in this house, both falling asleep and waking up to the soothing sounds of the waves crashing onto the shore.

Papa comes knocking on the side of our open bedroom door. "Ya'll ready?" His accent from growing up in Tennessee is thick, and I find myself wondering if I'd have one if we hadn't all moved to Colorado when I was really young.

"Yes!" Clara exclaims, and so marks the start of tradition number two. Go greet the ocean. Clara and I quickly slip on our sandals and drop all of our remaining luggage to the ground as we rush out the front door, Papa laughing behind.

"It's so warm!" I yell as Clara, Papa, and I are standing at the edge of the ocean while the waves meet our feet, slowly sinking us deeper into the sand. As we're standing there, breathing in the salty air for the first time in months, I think back to our earlier summers here.

"Papa, I'm sinking!" I would say as the sand swallowed up my toes, and then both my feet fully with each passing wave. Clara was so small standing next to me, the sinking sand was almost to her knees.

"You two better be careful! If you get stuck here, the sharks might come and getcha!" Papa said with a playful twinkle in his eye.

"Noooo!" Clara shouted before ripping her feet from the sand and running back towards the house. Papa and I were laughing as we continued to watch the sunset over the water.

This month. This place. It all holds so many wonderful memories and traditions. *A lot of those traditions are with Henry.* I look between Papa and Clara on either side and decide right then and there that no matter what happens tomorrow, or this summer, nothing will change how I feel about this place and moments like these. August has always promised traditions with family, and the special type of healing and peace that can only be provided by full days on the sand, under the sun, by the vast ocean that can make any problem instantly seem smaller. I trust August. I trust my family. I trust this place.

* * *

I wake up the next morning to the smell of bacon and freshly brewed coffee. *It doesn't get much better than this.* I try to wake up Clara, and am not surprised when she simply grunts and pulls the covers over her head. She's always up early to hit the road when coming here, but once she's here...she's in vacation mode for the rest of August. She'll sleep in most mornings. I give up and walk downstairs and into the kitchen to find Papa and Nana outside. I eye them through the screen doors that lead to our back patio. Papa sips his coffee while watching the water, while Nana is already engrossed in her book. I fix myself some coffee and pile my plate up with bacon, toast, and fruit before meeting them outside. At the sound of the sliding door opening, they both greet me with big smiles.

"Well, it's about time," Papa says as I slip into the chair next to him.

"Hey, you should be saying that to Clara; she's the one who refuses to wake up."

"Well, she better get on up, the waves are perfect for boogie boarding right now," he responds as he looks back out. I watch the waves coming in and close my eyes. Just as I am immersing myself in the sounds of the ocean and fully welcoming the day, Nana speaks up. "The Rollands should arrive here sometime around 4:30 p.m. today. I thought we could all have dinner together." I immediately feel a pit in my stomach at the anticipation of Henry getting here.

"Sounds great!" I respond, working up a smile before finishing my breakfast and going back to drag Clara out of bed.

"Ugh, okay! I'm up! I'm up!" Clara responds as I pull the covers off of her.

"Come on," I say, "Henry and Jules are getting here early this evening, and I just really want to enjoy having the ocean to ourselves before they get here." Clara is walking toward the bathroom to brush her teeth while I begin searching for a swimsuit to wear.

"You know," she responds, "Henry is like, basically in love with you, I'm sure he'll apologize for not writing, you'll give him crap about it, and then by the end of the night tonight, everything will be back to normal." I glare at her.

"Clara. He is not in love with me; you've got to stop with that. He's just my best friend. Or at least, I thought he was," I say as I rummage through my suitcase for my favorite black swimsuit.

Clara glares back at me before shutting the door to change. I sigh and face the bathroom door before responding. "Look, I just don't know what I'll say to him, okay. It just seems like his letter was trying to save face before having to actually see me in person. I feel like I changed a lot when we weren't talking. Maybe I changed because we weren't talking. He doesn't even know about anything that I've been dealing with. I don't know what to do. But, I do know that I don't want to talk about it anymore. Let's just enjoy today, just us. Okay?" There is silence behind the door for a minute before she opens it, dressed up in the cutest swimsuit and overalls with her hair tied up in a messy bun. Yet, she looks like she could be on the cover of a magazine. How she gets ready so effortlessly, I will never know.

"Okay." She says. "I won't say another word… if you buy me a coffee." I look at her dumbfounded, before I remember that I had completely promised to buy her our first coffee of the trip last week when she let me borrow her favorite dress.

I smile. "Okay. Deal. Now let's go, we're burning daylight!" We grab our boogie boards before rushing out the door, and I feel like a kid again for a moment as I shout to Papa and Nana, "Meet ya on the beach!"

* * *

Hours have passed, and we have all been under the sun, going back and forth from the ocean to our claimed spots on the sand. We started out boogie boarding, as Papa would take turns helping us catch the biggest wave. I remember when he taught us the first time. Clara was so small.

Papa used a big raft, riding the wave in with her and holding her tight. Now, here we all are as we look out at the never-ending water, trying to determine the best break in the wave and the perfect timing to catch the biggest one, stealing them from each other over and over again. Nana is on the beach under the umbrella. Every few minutes, I'll catch her looking up from her book and smiling as she watches us. I want to paint a picture of these moments in my mind forever. People change. Life throws curveballs, but family is forever, and these traditions look so beautiful and mean so much more as time passes. No matter how much time passes, nothing can take them away from me.

* * *

I don't know how long it's been as Clara and I get up from our now purposeless beach towels that are completely soaked and nearly covered in sand. Clara fell asleep while tanning as I escaped into my book, but eventually the sun became too bearing, and we decided to grab our boogie boards once again and head back into the waves. The current has not let up, and we are both watching in anticipation of the best one. I see the big blue building on the horizon, and I know that the next one coming could push me all the way to shore. Clara seems to sense it too, as she looks at me with wide eyes. We both position ourselves, stomachs flat on our boards, hands gripping the sides, and our backs turned to the forming wave. *I don't care how old I get, I will never outgrow this.* Within seconds, the wind shifts and the formation of the wave picks up, but significantly pushes towards my side. "No! I wanted to catch this one!" Clara shouts, but her voice fades quickly as the force of the wave slams into me and launches me towards the shore.

The wave is so powerful that it knocks my boogie board out from under me and leaves me tumbling underwater towards the bank. I hold my breath and wait it out, as this has happened time and time again. I do consider myself a professional boogie boarder at this point, if that's even a thing. As the wave coughs me up onto the shore, I immediately feel the salty water burning my nose. I'm facing the sand on all fours, trying to catch my breath.

"Wow. Now that was a big one. Care for some competition?" I freeze. I'd know that voice anywhere. No matter how many letters have been written, and how much time has gone by without hearing it. I look up between my now stringy salt-water filled hair that is partially in my eyes, and I see Henry Rolland looking down at me, one hand wrapped around his boogie board, the other extended out towards me.

3

Chapter Three

***

Henry looks the same, and yet different at the same time, as I stare up at him before reluctantly taking his hand to help me up. I steady myself and look back to see Clara swimming after my boogie board that is now further along the beach, being carried by the tide. I turn to look at Henry again, and I study him for the first time in over a year. I notice that his dark brown hair still curls out behind his ears, but it's a little longer and less put-together. His smile is the same, perfect teeth breaking through. Though as he smiles, I notice that it doesn't reach his eyes. There's a hollowness to them that wasn't there before. I don't know how long I've been assessing his facial features before he speaks up again.

"El? I was wondering if…"

"Elena! Sweetie, it's so good to see you!" I am immediately engulfed in the warmest hug from Henry's mom, and I am thankful for the interruption. I wrap my arms around her as tightly as I can to try to portray how much I love and feel for her. She was so close to her dad. *Henry was so close to his Grandpa.* I look him in the eyes as he stands behind Jules while I hug her. He gives me a half smile before dismissing himself to say hello to my Papa, and my Nana quickly trots over to me and Jules.

"Ohhhh! It has been too long!" She sings while joining us in the hug, now becoming one of the warmest feelings I've felt in a while.

"Um, hello, what about me?" Clara shouts as she tosses both of our boards onto the sand before folding herself into Nana's outstretched arm, welcoming her into the group hug.

This. I think to myself. *This is what I've needed all year. Nothing will ever change how it feels to be loved by these women.* I quickly wipe away a single tear that manages to escape before we finally let each other go and begin talking about dinner plans.

I overhear Papa and Henry already talking about fishing as I walk towards the house with just us girls.

"Oh, Clara dear," Jules says, "You'll meet Jason at dinner, he's my nephew, and he's been staying with us to help around the house with, you know…everything. He's around your age. I'm sure you two will get along well! He's a cutie…" She adds with a wink.

Clara laughs uncomfortably before looking at me with wide eyes behind Nana and Jules' backs. I wiggle my eyebrows up and down at her, which only causes her to roll her eyes before breaking off into a sprint, shouting, "Dibs on first shower!" I roll my eyes again before jogging behind her. *Some things never change.*

As I'm walking up the steps to the back patio, I look to my left and notice Henry sitting on the steps of their house next door, which is almost identical to ours, but coated in pastel blue paint. He's staring out at the ocean, seeming to be in deep thought. He looks over, as if sensing my stare, and locks his eyes with mine. I sigh. *Some things also change so quickly, and in the blink of an eye.*

I break eye contact as I march into the house and trot up the stairs as fast as I can to try and grab my things out of mine and Clara's shared bathroom to use the guest shower. I want to let the warm water run over my shoulders and get all of my deep shower thoughts out of the way before dinner. Another tradition we have is seating arrangements. And, if Henry sits in his designated seat next to mine, I am not sure how I will make conversation. It's been so long since we've spoken words to each other, let alone written. We used to be able to just know how the other person was feeling with the look of an eye, but his eyes weren't the same on the beach today. I wonder if our special language of unspoken words will work anymore, seeing that our written words have failed us.

* * *

Jules is both crying and laughing as Papa tells an old story about Grandpa Joe from many Augusts ago. I take a bite of the most delicious lasagna that Nana makes every year on the first night together with everyone, waiting in anticipation for the rest of the story. This is one of my favorites of our traditions. Eating together and sharing stories while catching up from the months we'd all been away. Although this time, it's been two summers since we've been in this room together like this. I look at Henry, who sits across the table from me. His cousin, Jason, had claimed the seat next to me before Henry even walked through the sliding doors into the dining area. Henry is picking at his food, another smile not reaching his eyes as he listens to Papa finish the story.

"He was trying so hard to show off on that old beat-up jet ski of his!

The two of you were so little, screaming for him to 'make more waves!' Papa continues, referring to me and Henry when we were younger. I look at Henry again, catching his eye briefly before looking back at my own plate of food.

"You two were begging, and he just couldn't resist. I remember him yelling for y'all to brace for impact before he whipped the jet ski around so fast, trying to splash y'all, only to completely fall off. You two thought it was some game, so you kept shouting for him to do it again and again. Eventually, he just kept faking as if he was falling off in so many different ways that just seemed entirely impossible!" Papa continues, "but the funniest part of it all was when the cops and paramedics walked up to us on the beach. Oh, your faces went white with fear, but Joe's went red with embarrassment."

I look at Jules, who's smiling while wiping a tear as she listens and stifles something that sounds like both a laugh and a choke of a sob. Then I look to Henry again, and when he looks at me, I give him a small smile. I know he misses him. I do too. Henry's mouth turns up at the corner as he looks back at me, with a half smile that almost reaches his eyes this time. *Almost.* We both look back at Papa.

"Someone on the balcony of a condo next to our houses had seen Joe fall and heard the fake yells and screams. They had called 911! Oh my, Joe was so embarrassed. He was red in the face explaining what was happening, and he got a good scolding." Papa laughs again. "Those officers and paramedics were in no mood to play around. I remember one of them saying in the most stern voice, 'Sir, this is the kind of horseplay we expect from teenagers. Not grown men. We don't have time to waste on tomfoolery like this." Papa's voice is deeper as he impersonates the officer before continuing the story, looking right at Henry.

"Your grandpa tried to put the blame on your mother! She was so mad, too!" Papa looks at Jules, whose face is a mixture of sadness, a scowl, and joy in her eyes. I once heard that grief and joy can co-exist. I guess this is what that looks like.

"Oh, he was a hoot!" Nana chimes in with her southern accent thick on the word *hoot*. Henry speaks up in a small voice while picking at his food again, eyes not leaving the pasta on his fork. "Yeah… he was."

* * *

After dinner, we are all helping clean up in the kitchen. Another tradition that allows us to all go get ice cream after. It used to be a tactic Nana and Jules used to get us kids to help with the dishes, and to this day, it still works. I'm handing a plate over to Jules to dry off before Nana hands me another dirty one. We have a system that works, and we stick to it every year. Clara and Nana scrape extra food into the trash. I rinse and wash, and then Jules dries everything before putting them back in their respective place. Henry and Papa are collecting the trash from the table in front of us. The men always end up with trash duty. Just as Henry is tying up his bag, Jules speaks up in a high-pitched voice, seeming to startle everyone.

"Oh, Henry, did you tell everyone your big news?"

Big news? I think to myself. *If he has big news, surely it can't be that big, right? He would have at least told me if something really big was happening in his life, wouldn't he? Then again, he did forget my birthday, and I didn't even tell him all of my news. Or, lack thereof. Did he not tell me because I haven't responded to his most recent letter before coming here?*

My thoughts are interrupted as Henry speaks up. "Mom, I wasn't really…" his face is red and panicked, and he quickly glances in my direction before Jules speaks up again.

"Henry was accepted into Universal Music Group's songwriting internship program in New York!"

Silence. There is silence that follows, or if people are reacting verbally, I simply can't hear them. I'm just staring at Henry, as he stares back at me.

"It's with Island Records! He leaves at the end of the summer for a whole year! I'll be so sad to see him go, but I'm so so proud of him."

It sounds like she's crying again, but I'm not sure. I'm not sure of anything right now as I look at Henry, studying his face again. He is attempting a smile at me, but this time, the hollowness in his eyes is back. It's a smile as if to say *sorry*. At least I think it is. I'm not sure if we can still read each other like that anymore. If he can still read me, then he would know by looking into my eyes right now that I am caught off guard, surprised, and confused more than ever. I don't know how much more change I can handle. I want to bury myself in our beach traditions for the rest of August and forget the world around us. But, as Henry dismisses himself out back to take out the trash, I realize that this August might be even different than the last.

4

Chapter Four

***

The sun is just starting to set as we all get ready to go to TCBY. In my personal opinion, it really is *The Country's Best Yogurt*.

"You kids have fun, we adults are going to stay here and chit chat before turning in early!" Jules exclaims while waving us off and tossing Henry the car keys. No matter how much time passes, when we're at this little slice of our perfect beach that's been painted by our memories, we will always be referred to as *the kids*.

I let Henry and Jason walk ahead as I pull Clara to the side.

"Call shotgun," I whisper. She eyes me with a look that says, *this is ridiculous,* before sighing and skipping over to catch up to the boys.

"Shotgun!" She sings before waiting by the passenger door for Henry to unlock it.

Henry looks as if he's about to protest before he unlocks the door and gets in the driver's seat without a word.

Henry drives on the most familiar and nostalgic road that leads to the creamiest frozen yogurt that I have been dreaming about since washing the first dish after dinner. There is only the sound of Drake playing in the background. He has always been a Drake fan, and I can't remember a time I was in a car with him and and one of his albums hasn't played. It's strange, though, because Henry's songwriting shows no influence from Drake. Henry's lyrics have always reminded me of *Fleetwood Mac* or even *The 1975* when he was going through his edgier phase of writing.

I miss when he used to share song ideas with me. His lyrics were always a way into his mind, as were my book ideas and poems that I'd share in my letters. I always looked forward to the little notes he'd leave in the margins when he'd mail it back, followed by his own work.

The sound of *Take Care* starting to play interrupts my thoughts. I look at Henry in the rearview mirror. This is usually a song that he can never refrain from singing along to, but he remains silent, lips formed in a tight line and eyebrows furrowed together as he focuses on the road ahead of him. Clara starts to make small conversation about the new construction of more condos near our house, an attempt to fill the awkward silence. Henry mumbles an "mhm" as she continues talking about the one that is being constructed straight ahead, going on and on about how it's supposed to have a lazy river, and we should sneak into it.

I consider chiming in, but then Henry makes eye contact with me in the rearview, to which I immediately look away and start a conversation with Jason. I ask him about South Carolina and his plans for college, and as he responds, he talks about his hope to take a backpacking trip through Europe for a year before interning with some tech company. I start to miss everything else he says, because I glance one more time, seeming to feel Henry's gaze. And when I look, his eyes immediately shift back to the road, as if I've caught him glancing at me at just the right second.

* * *

The bell chimes as I take the lead and open the spoon-shaped door, welcoming the smell of freshly made waffle cones and endless flavors of frozen yogurt. Clara and I march up to the glass casing to look at all the options, some bright and colorful, others rich and deep. We're wide-eyed as if we haven't been here a million times before. I feel Henry and Jason walk up behind us, but honestly, there is nothing that could break my focus from the desserts displayed in front of me. *This is one of the best traditions for sure.* My eye catches a vibrant blue case of yogurt, filled with Oreo cookie pieces.

"Can I please try a sample of the *Cookie Monster?*" I ask the young boy behind the counter who wears a colorful hat that's made to look like a waffle cone. He smiles before handing me a tiny spoon with the biggest sample you could fit onto it, which I appreciate as I taste the cookies and cream on my tongue. I don't know if the blue does anything else to the flavor. I'm sure it turns my mouth blue with one taste, but I don't even care because it's *that good.* I continue looking at the other options to see if there's anything else I want to try before I make my decision. It's a lengthy process every time, but if you don't take advantage of free samples at an ice cream shop, you're not doing it right in my opinion.

I see an option that says *Superman.* It looks like it may be Sorbet flavored. I ask for a sample of that one when Henry speaks up behind me.

"Every year you try nearly every sample, but you always end up choosing plain chocolate." I tense before turning around to face him and trying the new sample I now hold. *Yep, it was sorbet.*

"That may be true," I respond. "But people change. You should know." He looks taken aback as I turn around to order. "I'll take a scoop of the 'Cookie Monster,' please."

The boy behind the counter nods before scooping what looks like it could be two scoops into a small cup. While he does so, I look at the rich, dark chocolate yogurt nearby. *I wanted chocolate.*

We all take a seat at a round table, silent for the first couple of minutes as we enjoy our ice cream. Henry remains silent for the rest of our time here, but Jason carries the conversation as he talks more about his plans to backpack through Europe. It sounds really cool, and I'm shocked by how intrigued Clara seems in the conversation.

Or, maybe she's just intrigued by Jason.

I can never tell with her. She's always so closed off when it comes to guys. Maybe it's just the salt air that brings out this more relaxed vibe from her. It usually does that for me, but as I watch Henry walk over to throw away his now-empty cup, shoulders slumped over, I realize that we'll need to talk about things soon, or else August will not be the relaxing reset we both need.

When we get back into the car, Clara suggests that we all go to the fishing pier. This is another tradition I love. I remember the first time our Papa took me here when Clara was too little to be surrounded by flying fish hooks in every direction. We walked along the wooden pier for what felt like miles to me, just the two of us, until we reached the end and were met with the dark ocean waves underneath and fishermen all waiting patiently on the sides, lines cast over. One year, someone caught a small shark. I remember thinking it was the coolest thing I had ever seen. Each year since then, Papa and I have gone together to see if someone else gets lucky enough to catch one. No one has since then. But we will always go together nevertheless. I'll have to make sure I plan to go with him this trip, even though we're all going now.

"Sounds good to me," Jason responds to Clara. "I'd love to see if anyone catches anything good."

Henry simply nods in response before turning right and heading towards the pier. As he does, my phone vibrates in my back pocket.

Clara: You two have GOT to talk.

I look at Clara in the rearview mirror and simply nod before I begin contemplating what I will say. For the first time ever between Henry and I, I'm not sure how to express how I'm feeling to him. For the first time, I'm at a loss for words, and I run out of time to figure it out as we pull into the parking lot.

* * *

Clara leads Jason ahead of Henry and I as we begin down the straight path of the pier. It's dark now, but the lights illuminate the walkway and reflect off the water below. The waves are crashing against the beams that hold everything in place. It smells like salt water and fish, which is more comforting than one would think.

It smells like memories.

I know Clara is purposefully walking ahead of Henry and I. I begin to wonder what she and Jason are talking about when I should really be figuring out how to start a conversation with Henry right now. I could go with small talk, but I think he and I both know we've never been good at that. We used to have to pause to take breaths when talking to each other. We always had so much to say. I'm about to speak up and apologize for my *slightly* petty comment at the yogurt shop when Henry shouts from beside me.

"Whoa Whoa Whoa!"

In a blur, I am pushed to the side, Henry now to the left of me, hand held up in the air as if to block me from something. Before I know it, I see the hook pierce his hand, and I cringe as he winces in pain. I quickly look at the fisherman, who turns around wide-eyed.

"Ah, shoot, man!" He shouts before rushing up to us. Henry is focused on his now bloody hand, trying to assess the damage.

"Oh brother, I am so sorry," the man speaks up again, his eyes crinkling as he too starts to assess Henry's hand. He looks older, but not withered. His eyes are youthful as he continues talking. "This is my first time at this pier. I'm not used to so many people being around; I should have been paying more attention."

The man seems like he's genuinely sorry. I look behind him to see a young girl with nearly white blonde hair peeking over at us, slightly startled. She looks to be about the age I was when my Papa took me here the first time. Nostalgia tugs at my heart.

Henry removes the hook from his hand gently with the man's help, and my hand instinctively places itself on Henry's shoulder as he winces again. I feel him relax instantly when I do.

"I'll drive us to an urgent care. You should get that cleaned and disinfected." I say as the man hands Henry a handkerchief.

"Oh, I can take you there, it's my fault I should."

I look behind the man and see the little girl still watching. She has a little pink fishing rod next to her. "No," I say in response. "It's fine really, we can take care of it," I say, and gesture towards the little girl.

The man seems to pick up on my way of saying, *take care of her.* His youthful eyes sparkle as he puts a hand over his heart.

"Thank you really, ah…" He scrambles and pulls a gum wrapper and a pen from his blue jean pocket. "Here's my number, please reach out to me and let me know how everything turns out, or if y'all need anything." He looks at Henry as he says that last part.

"We will. Enjoy the rest of your fishing… just be careful." I add with a smile.

He nods and tips his hat before walking back over to the little girl. She smiles widely at him as he kneels down to her level. I don't realize I'm watching their interaction so intently until Henry clears his throat next to me.

"El, I realize exactly what you're thinking right now. Nostalgia and all, but um, I am kinda losing blood here..."

I snap my head to him quickly. "Oh my gosh, okay, yeah let's go, give me the keys."

He uses his uninjured hand to fish the keys from his pocket. As he sets them in my hand, I feel that warm nostalgic feeling again. But this time, it doesn't come from the little girl and her dad. It comes from the fact that Henry knew. He knew exactly what was going through my mind while I watched their interaction. Maybe things haven't changed as much as I thought.

5

Chapter Five

* * *

Henry and I quickly walked to the car while I simultaneously texted Clara to explain what happened. She responded before we even made it to the car.

Clara: We'll wait here. TALK to him.

I'm now driving to the nearest urgent care, which is only five minutes away, but as I glance over at Henry and his now bloody, wrapped hand, I begin to get queasy and step on the gas a little more. I tense up, shoulders pushed forward as I hunch over the steering wheel and look ahead to make sure I don't miss a turn. Henry shuffles next to me, and I can feel his stare.

"El…it's fine, seriously. I mean I can already tell I won't need stitches, they'll clean it up quickly, and I'll be good as new."

I look over at his hand again before quickly turning my eyes back to the road. "Okay, yeah, but that doesn't change the fact that your hand is bloody."

He keeps his gaze locked on me. "Okay, El, you're looking a little pale, more so than usual. Just relax."

I glare at his comment about my paleness. I've taken after my dad's side of the family. This meant that I was the odd one out, starting with my nearly white blonde hair, followed by the only evidence of the sun on my skin, which are my many freckles and inevitable sun burns that I tend to get every summer. Meanwhile, everyone else around me gets golden bronzed, especially Clara. Henry catches onto my glare, again seeming to read my mind with one look as he responds.

"Hey, maybe this summer you'll get lucky and finally get sun-kissed instead of brutally burned."

I glare at him harder as he continues. "Remember three summers ago when you fell asleep outside and your whole face swelled?" He laughs. I glare quickly, yet again, before focusing back on the road. "I'm sure it was so not fun for you, but I have pictures that will forever be so funny to look back on. I'm sorry, but you looked so funny."

He's holding in laughter while looking at me, seeming to wait for approval to continue laughing. I remember that sunburn, one of my worst yet. But I also remember the pictures, and I did look pretty ridiculous. I let out a short huff of a laugh, and he takes it as his signal to join in. I know he's just trying to distract me from my anxiety, and when I see the urgent care straight ahead, I realize it worked. Even after all this time spent not speaking, he still knows how to read me and meet me right where I am in my mind, without me even having to say a word. I'm glad.

I pull into the urgent care and turn off the car. I know he's still looking over at me before I turn and meet his gaze. Our eyes lock, and I can tell his mind is running wild with thoughts. I can tell there's something he wants to say, and as his lips part to speak, I motion towards his now blood-soaked, wrapped hand.

"I think I might wait in the car," I say. "If that's okay." Henry closes his mouth, seeming to understand that now is not the time to have the conversation I know he's been trying to have with me since I quite literally washed up on the shore in front of him earlier this afternoon. *It feels like today has been a week already. My mind is running wild.*

"Yeah, that's fine. I'll be right back." Henry smiles before getting out of the car.

I watch him walk in until I can no longer see him, and then I start the car again, turning the air on full blast, before sinking into my seat and resting my eyes for a moment. I don't know what this impending conversation with Henry will bring. I don't know how he'll explain seemingly falling off the face of the earth and ignoring my every letter for so long. In the midst of not knowing a lot, though, I do know that it will bring up things that I am not ready to open up about. Things that do not belong in this escape from reality that is August. I do know that he'll ask me questions about my year and how I've been. *And, I know he'll see straight through me if I lie and say that I'm fine.*

* * *

We get back to the house after picking up Clara and Jason, and I immediately go upstairs to change into my swimsuit. Something about a good night swim always seems to clear my head. Henry's hand seemed fine, no stitches needed or anything. The car ride back was mostly silent, aside from Clara singing along to Taylor Swift, which caused both guys in the back to keep to themselves. I would usually sing along, but I just drove, completely stuck in my head. I know Henry and I need to talk more, but I just can't shake the feeling that things between us are different.

I change into my favorite blue bikini from Aerie, grab my beach towel, and head downstairs to the pool. There's one in between both of our beach houses that my grandparents and Henry's family went in on together when we were all younger. I remember the day we drove up for the summer, and I eyed the pool as soon as we pulled into the driveway. They had it built for us during the school year, and it was a huge surprise. Tonight, I am hoping that I am the only one with the need for a night swim. I open the gate that surrounds the pool and place my towel on a chair before deciphering whether I want to fully jump in or just slowly make my way into the water. I stick one foot in at the stairs to test out the temperature, and it's perfect. It's just warm enough after a day reflecting the rays of the sun. I jump into the deep end and let myself fully submerge, releasing all of my breath as I float to the bottom. *Silence.*

These few short moments under the water are when my thoughts can't get the best of me. All I can focus on is holding my breath and feeling the weights lift off my shoulders as I become instantly lighter, floating through the water.

I'm about to come up for air when I feel a sudden shift in the water and the sound of a splash.

Suddenly, I no longer feel weightless.

I come up and wipe my eyes, only to be met with Henry's gaze back at me. I notice his shoulders and how broad they are now. Definitely more pronounced than the last time I saw him. I must not have noticed this earlier. *Although I don't see how.* His brown curls are now completely straight, making his wet hair look longer. The moonlight reflects off his collarbone and into his deep brown eyes, making them look lighter. I'm not sure how long I've been staring at him, but he hasn't said anything as he looks back. I decide to speak up while I look away.

"Can you get your hand wet?" I swim towards the ledge beneath the fountain at the far end of the pool and take a seat, Henry now a blurry picture behind the waterfall in front of me. Distance between us.

"Yeah, they said it wasn't that serious, really just had to disinfect it, that's all." His voice grows closer, and he comes into clearer vision, swimming up towards the waterfall. I don't know why, but I feel my heart begin to beat faster as he gets closer. *What is this? Anxiety?*

"Oh, that's good," I respond as his head breaks through the waterfall. He's now positioned inches away from me. His wet hair falls into his face, and water droplets now rest on his shoulders that are highlighted perfectly by the moonlight. Before I know what I'm saying, I ask, "Have you been working out?"

The side of his mouth twitches. "Yeah, actually, it's been like my main source of therapy since Grandpa Joe…" My heart breaks a little before he continues. "I started going sometime after his funeral, right around the same time I stopped writing back." I break my gaze from his. As I do, I feel his hand reach out to touch the backside of my arm that rests beneath the water.

"El, I'm so sorry. I didn't mean to hurt you, and I know that I did. I can tell. But when I lost Grandpa, I don't know. I feel like I lost a piece of myself. I mean, besides you, he really was my best friend. He knew me inside and out, and usually when I would wait to hear back from you as we wrote, I would confide in him. It was just so sudden, El, I didn't know how to deal. So for a while, I just didn't."

I meet his gaze and continue to let him speak. "I started going to the gym, and that helped, but only while I was there. When I left, I went right back into this funk I couldn't get out of. My grades slipped, and I couldn't even write songs, let alone write to you. And, the more time that went on, the guiltier I felt about so many things. There was also the stress my mom felt as things between my dad and I became more tense without Grandpa there to defend me. It just all made me struggle to figure out what to even say to you. I was ashamed. There was a period when I couldn't even keep track of what day of the week it was. That is until my mom asked me if I had wished you a happy birthday."

He looks down, ashamed. "El, I am so sorry. I am still working on coming out of this funk, I really am. I couldn't be there for myself, let alone anyone else. But, I'm not going to make any more excuses." He looks deep into my eyes. His are sorrowful and the deepest brown that is easy to lose yourself in. I don't know if I've ever seen his eyes this up close before.

"I know I messed up. I hope I didn't ruin the best thing I've had in my life. Your friendship is everything to me. I'd hate to think I messed that up."

I'm still lost in his eyes, soaking in everything that he just said, everything he's been through.

Everything I've been through this year that he has no idea about. The fact that there's still the looming topic of his internship that I don't even want to ask him about right now comes to the surface of my mind. I used to be able to feel like I could ask him anything, but now… I am just at a loss for words. The longer I look, the faster my heart beats still, and I really can't understand why. Even though I've been hurt and nervous about talking to him, I have never once felt this type of nervousness around him. I blame it on the fact that he does look really good, and he must know it. I know he's waiting for any type of response, and I know that I need to take a breather, get out from under this fountain, *from under his gaze*, and talk to him more when the sun comes up.

"El?" His voice knocks me out of my trance. "Did I ruin our friendship?"

Before I know what I'm doing, I run a hand through his wet hair. His eyes shut at the touch of my hand.

"You damaged it," I say as I rest my hand on his shoulder now. His eyes open, and they look hollow again before I say, "But nothing is so damaged that it can't be fixed."

With that, his eyes begin to have life in them again as a smile reaches them. I give a shy smile back before turning around and hauling myself out of the pool. I quickly grab my towel, wrap myself up, and make my way in for the night. When I look back as I open the back door to my house, I see him now sitting in the spot I was, under the waterfall, still smiling, and looking out onto the water. As I make my way upstairs into the bathroom, I smile too, but I don't realize how much I am also blushing until I look in the mirror.

6

Chapter Six

* * *

"Henry! No!" I shouted as he chased me around the pool. He was trying to push me in. Grandpa Joe was laughing as he sat in a poolside chair with his red bucket hat and overalls. The classic Grandpa Joe look.

"Oh, fiddle! How do I get this thing to record?" He messed with his brand-new iPhone that he switched to just last month. Before this, it was strictly flip phones or nothing. The sliding door opened, and Jules walked out onto the patio.

"Julie, help me with this here, I wanna get these rascals on film."

Jules laughed as she walked over to help her dad record Henry and me. Henry grabbed my arm, but I easily slipped out of his grip since I had just applied a thick layer of spray-on sunscreen.

"Ha!" I said as his eyes widened. He definitely thought that he had me there, and I relished in watching as he realized his mistake, while his hand still reached out for me, and he lost his balance and fell into the pool himself.

34

I jumped in victory and laughed. Henry's head bobbed back up, and his eyes glared at me. "Oh, you're so gonna pay for that," he threatened as he hauled himself out of the pool.

"El, can I have a huuuggg?" He sang as he walked towards me, dripping wet, while I was fully clothed, and in my favorite lilac summer dress, might I add.

"Oh, nuh uh, don't you dare, Henry!" I ran away from him and busted through the gate. My feet were sinking in the sand and slowing me down as I bolted towards the beach.

"You two are making me lose my breath, I can't stop laughing!" Grandpa Joe shouted while Henry chased after me. "You'll all get to look back on this one day. I got it on video! Memories are everything."

"Careful, you two, it's about to get dark out!" Jules yelled after us.

I was running down the beach, the sun had just started to set, and I lost my breath at the beauty of it, along with the fact that my heart was beating fast from running. I was lost in the vibrant and warm colors of the sky when two wet arms wrapped around my waist. I shrieked as Henry lifted me off the ground and spun me in a circle.

"Gotcha!"

We both laughed until we fell down. We lay beside each other, the sand beneath my back felt as soft as a bed. I could have drifted off to sleep there. And, I think that I do, until...

I smell pancakes, my senses waking up the rest of my body almost immediately. As I turn over, the sandy bed I was lying in next to Henry just moments ago, turns into my bed. I let out a sigh. It had felt so real. I wish it were. *I wish Grandpa Joe were still here, and that I could really watch the video he took.*

* * *

I throw off my blanket and immediately put on my slippers. I'm thankful that the smell of pancakes was not a part of my dream. Another tradition. Nana makes Cracker Barrel pancakes with their special mix, and nothing can ever compare. I quickly finish my morning bathroom routine and skip downstairs.

"I smell pancakes!" I sing as I round the corner into the kitchen. I stop immediately when I see that Henry is flipping pancakes over the stove where Nana would usually be. I rub my eyes and look again. *Yep, it's him.*

"Oh! Good, you're up! They're almost ready." He says, looking at me for a brief second before adjusting the heat of the stove and placing a pancake atop a rather high stack already.

"Hey, um, where is everyone else?" I pad over to the bar stools and take a seat before noticing coffee has already been brewed. Henry sees me eyeing the pot, reads my mind, and fixes a mug for me. He places it in front of me before walking to the fridge and grabbing my favorite oat milk caramel creamer, and setting it next to my mug. *He still knows me better than anyone else.*

"Thanks," I mutter as I start to pour the creamer and taste-test until it's the perfect blend of coffee with a hint of caramel.

"Well, Jason and I woke up super early to go for a run on the beach, and when mom saw we were headed out, she mentioned that she and your grandparents wanted to go out for breakfast together. I told them to go ahead, and that Jason and I could handle breakfast over here. I figured they might enjoy some time out together, and I also figured you and Clara would want to sleep in. So I just decided to take over and have breakfast made by the time you two woke up."

"Oh, well, thanks." I try to think of something else to say to fill the awkward silence. "Where is Jason anyway?" I ask.

"He just ran to the store to get syrup, we were out. Is Clara up yet?"

I laugh. "Oh, definitely not. It's 9:30, so she's still got about two more hours until she's fully slept in to her liking."

Henry's jaw drops. "Wow, I thought she would've outgrown that. College will be a rude awakening for her next year. I remember it was for you." He looks over at me. There's a playful glimmer in his eyes that I haven't seen in over a year. *I missed it.*

"Hey, I am better about it now, okay. And, also, I don't want to think about her leaving for college yet."

Not after I just moved home, am completely out of a job, and all of my friends have moved far away.

I stare into my coffee mug and then look back up at Henry. His gaze is fixed on me again. "I'm sorry I didn't…"

"I'm back with the goods!" Jason interrupts.

Henry gives me a softened look, to which I respond with a shrug and a weak smile. Jason walks into the kitchen and places the bag of groceries on the counter.

"I also got some strawberries from this fruit stand, too. Couldn't pass it up."

"Mmm, that sounds good. Clara will love that." I say, and immediately notice Jason's eyebrows raise at the mention of her name. He looks around, as if to check and see if she's down here.

"Where is Clara anyway? Did she decide to go to the beach early or something? I haven't seen her all morning."

Henry and I look at each other and break into a laugh, leaving Jason confused. He can't pick up on what we've just communicated with one simple look. No one can. *Just us. Just like before.*

* * *

"MMMMHM! These pancakes are soooo good!" Clara exclaims as she stabs a fork in another one from the pile before drowning it in more syrup on her plate. I laugh, and catch Jason's eyes on her. He seems to be admiring her, while Clara is admiring her pancakes. I look at Henry, who seems to have caught on to this, too. He notices that I have also noticed, and we give each other a knowing look before he speaks up.

"Hey, Clara, Jason was telling me he wants to learn how to boogie board properly. Believe it or not, he's never been one for water, but he said it looks fun. Would you wanna teach him while I start cleaning up after breakfast? The waves look perfect today." Henry eyes me as if to communicate that he's trying to get them alone. I look at Jason, his eyes are hopeful on Clara while she is trying to finish chewing her food to respond.

"Oh! I can help you clean up, too, Clara, you should teach him!" I look at her as I say this, and she seems taken aback. I knew she wouldn't say no, though, because she's been wanting Henry and me to talk since before he even got here. But, it's funny to see her somewhat flustered and seeming to realize just what Henry and I are doing. Once my sister turned fourteen, Henry and I would have fun every summer playing matchmaker for her. She hated it, but every teenage boy on the beach would notice her, I mean, who wouldn't with her perfectly bronzed skin, deep brown eyes, and dark hair that cascaded effortlessly in waves past her shoulders. Boys would always try to approach her before approaching us to ask about her after she'd brushed them off. Nothing ever came of anything, and she always turned the guys down, but now that I'm suspecting Jason is interested in her, I'm eager to play matchmaker again. Just another tradition, only it's one of mine and Henry's.

Clara takes a sip of water, side eyes Henry and me without Jason noticing, and then says in a cheery and unbothered voice, "Sure! I'm done if you wanna go now. Boogie boards are already out front, you can use Elena's."

Jason's face lights up as he nods, finishing his orange juice in one gulp before following Clara out the back sliding doors that lead to our beach access. As soon as the door closes, Henry starts laughing. I grin while I walk over to fill up my coffee mug for the second time.

"Oh man, El, Jason has got it bad. He thinks Clara's the 'most beautiful girl I've ever seeeen, man!'" He says the last part, whining, seemingly impersonating Jason.

I laugh. "Did he really say that? Well, good luck to him. Clara's a hard one to impress." I say as I set the coffee pot back down and take a sip of my now perfectly warm and refreshed drink. *The smell of coffee.* I need it to fill my future house every morning. Something about it just wakes up my senses before I even take a sip. The smell of freshly brewed coffee feels like a warm hug of a blanket on a rainy day with the perfect book. The smell of freshly brewed coffee indicates the start of a day, so it feels like new beginnings. Motivation. Henry's voice interrupts my daydream about coffee.

"What are you thinking about?" At some point between my comment about Clara and my fixation on my drink, he stood up and made his way over to me. His hand reaches behind me and rests on the edge of the counter that my back is now leaning on. My heart rate increases again, like in the pool under the waterfall just last night.

"Honestly? I was daydreaming about my love for coffee," I say as I take another sip.

He shakes his head. "Same old El."

His eyes are staring deep into mine now. So many things need to be said, but here we are again. Just observing each other, wondering what's behind our eyes, and what's happened between us, what's changed, after all this time.

"Why didn't you tell me about your internship?" I blurt out.

His head drops as he eyes the floor. "I don't know. I found out after I sent you the most recent letter, and when you didn't write back... I don't know. I just figured that you didn't want to hear from me."

I shake my head. "Henry, that letter. I mean, after all those months, you just brushed off shutting me out and going M.I.A. You apologized for it like you forgot to give me back one of my favorite books you borrowed for a really long time or something. Or like you only failed to write me for two weeks… not nearly nine months. I didn't know what to say to that either." He looks hurt. "You passed your writer's block on to me," I say as a light joke to try and ease some of the hurt that I see behind his eyes from my accusation. He tries to smile, but the hurt is still evident in his attempt. He nods his head briefly in understanding as his eyes meet mine again. Both of his arms are outstretched on either side of me as his palms rest on the counter. I don't even know if he realizes that he's trapped me in. His eyes won't leave mine.

"Have you still been writing?" He asks, obviously trying to change the subject of the internship, which I will most definitely circle back around to when I'm not stuck between both of his… now broad arms.

"Um. Well, actually. I quit my job, so not recently, no." I'm now looking at the floor as I say this.

"El… I'm so sorry. What happ… I mean, you don't have to talk about it if you don't want to. You're so talented, okay? El.. look at me."

I hesitate, but slowly bring my head up. I'm met with the deepest brown yet again. His eyes seemingly still bright in the midst of the pain that lay behind them.

"Look. You didn't like writing for them anyway. You had no freedom with what you wrote. You never felt like you had a voice. Now, you can write what you want. No one can stop you."

I nod and close my eyes. He's right. I hated that job. Writing with such limitations about things I didn't care about? It felt like a cage. Little does he know, quitting my job was the least of the things that have been bothering me and hindering my writing.

"It's their loss, okay?" I open my eyes as he says this. "I would know. Losing you… even just for a little while…you leave an absence that no other person, place, or thing can fill. They'll notice that. I did."

Tears brim in my eyes. I want to tell him about everything else. About my friends leaving. About how utterly lonely I have felt. But I don't want to talk about those things here. Not yet. Those problems don't exist here. They stay at home. But on this beach. In this house. *With my best friend.* With our families and our traditions, and the ocean that stays exactly where it is, never failing to greet us with beautiful waves and memories it will hold forever, nothing can take that away. Not if I don't let it. Not if I pretend that reality doesn't exist outside of our own little world we make here every summer.

I'm desperate for relief from this heavy conversation. Henry's eyes are still fixed on mine. He seems lost in them, or deep in thought. I take this as my opportunity to strike. I act as if I'm turning around to grab the coffee pot again to top off my mug, which is a completely believable act from me. Three cups are nothing. However, instead of reaching for the mug, I quickly dunk my hand into the bag of powdered sugar that Henry had used to dust on top of our pancakes. I turn around, hold my hand out, and blow. Henry's eyes squeeze shut as he braces for the impact. His whole face is now coated with the white dusting of sugar. I can't help myself. I burst out in a fit of laughter.

"There. Now all is forgiven. We're even." I say as he wipes his eyes and licks around his mouth to simultaneously taste and clean off some of the sugar. I turn around to grab more before his massive arms reach around me and slam the bag shut on the counter, causing a cloud of powder to explode into my face. I gasp.

"No." He says. "Now, we're even." I feel his breath on the back of my neck as he whispers this.

"Oh my gosh, you did not! Henry, I'm gonna break out!"

He starts laughing now. I try to pry his hand off the top of the bag. As I do so, I lose my breath when his other arm wraps around my waist and pulls me away from the counter. I shriek. His other powder-sugar-coated arm wraps around the other side of me, and before I know it, I'm swung around to face away from the counter.

"Henry!" I shout. His grip is not letting up. My heart is beating fast. I'm trying to break free, screaming and laughing. I finally manage to turn around in his grip, and we both stop making any noise instantly altogether. My breath catches in my throat. His hands are now clasped together, resting at the small of my back. Mine are wrapped behind his neck. His gaze. His striking deep gaze is not moving from mine. I catch him looking down at my lips before we hear the door unlock. He immediately releases me from his grip and steps back.

"We're back!" Nana calls as she walks into the kitchen, only to gasp out loud at the sight of us.

"What is it?" I hear Jules say behind her before she sees what Nana is staring at. Us. With fully coated faces of powdered sugar, and even more on the floor and cabinets. I look around at the mess. I guess the whole bag must have fallen off the counter when Henry grabbed me and pulled me from it. I look at Henry. We're both fighting back laughter, but I can see it all behind his eyes. Pure joy. I feel like we're nine years old again. *No wonder they still refer to us as kids every summer.*

Jules sighs. "Ladies and gentlemen, my grown son who's about to live on his own in one of the biggest cities in the world. You'd think he'd have learned by now."

Her voice is playful, but I watch the light leave Henry's eyes. I feel the child-like joy slip away from me, as reality hits us both, reminding us that we aren't kids, we never would be again, and the real world still awaits us with its pressure and expectations. This is not supposed to happen here. Not in this little slice of our beach. Things are supposed to always be the same here.

"I'll get to cleaning," Henry says in a monotone voice. I move to start helping him, but don't say anything as I am lost in my thoughts. *Maybe this place will never change, but we inevitably will. Maybe we already have.*

7

Chapter Seven

***

A silence has fallen between Henry and me as I put the last dirty dish back up in the cabinet. It's obvious our brief moment back to normalcy between us is over as Henry refuses to meet my eyes while he finishes wiping down the counters. The only sound to be heard is Jules and Nana on the couch talking about potential places for Henry to live in the city.

He has a plan. What do I have? Aspiration? Sure. But what's aspiration without a plan?

Before I can overthink about the unknowns of my future any longer, the back door slides open and laughter fills the room. Jason and Clara are laughing and absolutely dripping wet as they stumble in, boogie boards at each of their sides.

"Now, get some towels! Don't track water in the house!" Nana and Jules hop off the couch to go get towels, I assume, but my gaze is fixed on the interaction happening in front of me. Clara is wringing out her saltwater-filled hair, and Jason is staring at her as if he's mesmerized by the action. Clara speaks up while he continues to not break from his gaze.

"You guys should have seen him!" She places a hand on his shoulder while she speaks. This is strange. Clara hates physical touch. She would barely let me hug her after she had gotten home from a month-long trip to a different beach in Florida with her best friend a couple of summers back. She starts laughing again. Her hand has not moved.

"The biggest wave ever just came out of nowhere, and Jason's back was turned to it!" Her grip on his shoulder tightens as she laughs harder, and I think I see Jason tense a little at the touch. "It just completely swallowed him and knocked his hat off! By the time he came up, his hat was moving down the beach and out to sea! We had to swim after it, but then he got hit by another wave! He just could not catch a break!" She laughs again and looks over at him. I watch her as she registers that he's clearly been eyeing her like that for some time now. I also see the moment she glances at her hand gripping his shoulder, to which she then pats it.

"Definitely needs more lessons," she says before excusing herself to the bathroom. When she exits, Henry and I share a knowing glance, and when we look at Jason, he seems to pick up the communication behind our eyes.

"Yeah, uh, I'm gonna go shower," Jason says before walking out the back door. I look over at Henry again. He's still looking at me, and I know he wants to say something. Two summers ago, this would have been something we debriefed over immediately. We would play matchmaker and have fun concocting plans to set them up or embarrass them. Harmless pranks. But he simply blows out a sigh and says he's going to go finish unpacking. When he's gone, I am still frozen behind the kitchen counter, replaying the short moments ago when his arms were wrapped around me briefly, and our laughter filled the air. I want to save each of these moments in a jar and lock it up tight so I'll always have them, because I fear I'm running out.

* * *

By the time Clara is finished getting ready for bed, I'm already tucked in tight and ready to drift off into a deep slumber. Just as I can feel myself on the verge of sleep, I also feel a big dip in my bed as Clara lands next to me, quickly grabbing my other pillow and hitting it over my head.

"Ugh! Clara, what?" I grumpily ask as I sit up abruptly and turn on the bedside lamp.

"I need to know what's up with the weirdness between you and Henry now. Did you guys end up talking? Because at this point, it's getting ridiculous. You guys are best friends, surely you both can talk things through. I've noticed the shift, too, and I want things to go back to normal."

I sigh. "Well, yeah, we kind of talked. He told me about what was going through his head when he had stopped writing. We touched on his internship just a little bit, but…something has still shifted between us, and I can't figure it out. We like, almost had a moment in the pool the other day, and then again this morning in the kitchen…" I feel the heat rising on my cheeks as I verbally acknowledge this for the first time. Clara raises one eyebrow.

"A moment? Uh, define *moment*? Did he finally confess his undying love for you? If so, it's about time…"

"No!" I cut her off. "No, Clara, this is not that. It's never been that, and even if there was a chance it could be… there's not enough time to figure that out before he leaves, and who knows if he'll ever talk to me again when he does go? He's gone over nine months without speaking to me, I'm sure he could go longer."

"Elena… come on. I know you feel it too. I've lived with you long enough to see it. Why do you think you care so much? Why do you think you've turned down every guy that has ever remotely been interested in you, or always found something wrong with them? I'll tell you what's wrong with them. They're not Henry… and deep down you know he's the one you really want."

I have no response to this. I've never let myself open that door in the back of my mind that may or may not lead to unresolved feelings for my best friend. It's too complicated, and it's obviously too late. If he felt that way, he wouldn't have so easily been able to cut me out of his life for nearly a year. No. I am mentally bolting that door locked to keep it shut in the back of my mind, where it belongs.

"Enough about me, what about the way Jason was so obviously gawking over you today, huh?" Clara rolls her eyes and immediately gets off my bed and stomps over to hers, dismissing my question. *Two can play at this game.*

"Yeah, no. I'm not even gonna let you go there tonight. There's nothing even there, and I see what you did there. I'll give you a pass for tonight because I'm exhausted." She tucks herself in, and I reach over to turn off the lamp. "Coffee tomorrow morning?"

I smile in the now fully dark room. No matter what happens in this life with friends or lovers or anyone, the bond between my sister and me will never be broken. I am hers. She is mine. We are each other's in this life through every season, and August is still ours.

"Of course. You read my mind." I say through a yawn before finally drifting off to sleep, hoping my dreams bring more memories of Augusts passed.

* * *

The waves today are the perfect ones for boogie boarding. They're the type that have swells reaching over my head just before they curl over and break, launching me forward and up as they carry me to shore. They're coming one after another now as I sit next to Nana and Jules, the three of us all reading with the sound of the waves crashing in front of us. I ended up ingesting way too much saltwater as the waves did not let up, and I opted to take a break. I look up briefly from the page I'm currently reading, and find Clara trying to teach Jason how to catch the wave that's forming behind them. She's laughing again. Something is brewing there, I just know it, but I don't know if Clara even knows it herself.

Looking over to my left, I see Henry and Papa adjusting their fishing rods, adding more bait. Henry's smile reaches his eyes as he laughs at something Papa says. It's nice to see him this way. I'm glad my family can fill the smallest part of the biggest hole that Grandpa Joe left. Looking out into the water now, I think of him and how he used to help me collect seashells and chase me with the sand fleas he'd find that still gross me out to this day. I know that if he saw this sight before him right now, he'd smile so hard before telling us we need to reapply sunscreen. He was always the one to be on top of that, and I'm just wondering which one of us will get burned first. My money's on Clara.

Just as I'm about to bury my nose back into my book, I notice she and Jason are now coming out of the water. They're making their way over to our chairs when two guys who have been sitting close by walk over to them. I don't recognize them from past summers. Maybe they're first-timers. I watch Clara and Jason both laugh before looking at each other and nodding their heads. The taller guy on the right takes Jason's phone, I assume to exchange numbers, and with a thumbs up, both guys walk back over to their chairs, fold them up, and walk away. Clara immediately walks over to her towel as Jason heads towards Henry and Papa. I look at Clara expectantly for an explanation, to which she nods her head for me to come join her. I mark my place in my book and jump up to sit next to her on her towel.

"Okay, what was that about? Did those guys hit on you or something? Why did he have Jason's phone?" I pause before adding, "The tall blonde one was kind of cute." I make myself comfy on her towel, and she readjusts, sitting up more as if preparing to answer all of my questions.

"I know! He looked like some surfer guy you'd find on an Abercrombie & Fitch poster!" The image too easily comes to my mind. *He so did.*

"So apparently they're both brothers," Clara continues. "They've rented out a beach house a few houses down from ours, and they're throwing a grad party tonight for his younger brother's high school graduation. The blonde one is older, but the younger one is about to start college, which honestly works for me." She laughs. "But anyway, they invited all of us! They want me, you, Henry, and Jason to come. They said that they bought way too much food, and they want to invite the locals. Of course, he thought we were locals, I mean, we basically are at this point. But what do you say? This could be sooo fun. It can be like my grad party, too, except on the beach!"

I ponder at Clara's pleading eyes. She's begging because she knows I'm not one for parties. But it does sound fun, and honestly, I wouldn't mind seeing that guy again. He really was like a real-life Ken doll.

"Okay," I say. "Let's do it, but we need to wait until all the adults are asleep or they'll just ask question after question."

Clara nods and simultaneously squeals. "Yes! Okay, let's hit a couple more waves and then go in and pick out outfits!" I laugh as she pulls me up forcefully by one arm. We grab our boogie boards and run towards the water.

"Oh! And they said there's an infinity pool, so we HAVE to bring our bathing suits!" An infinity pool sounds so cool. I've never heard of a house down here having one of those. I mean, our house is super nice, but it's definitely outdated. This one must be more modern and new. I wonder how these guys could afford to rent it.

Clara and I turn our backs from the swells forming, occasionally looking back to try and catch the one with the most potential. I look over to where Jason and Henry are on the shore, Papa having walked back towards Nana and Jules. Jason is using his hands, pointing over to where the two brothers once sat, as he talks to Henry. He then points to us, and as he does, Henry looks our way, locking eyes with me for just a moment before giving a half smile and nodding briefly while turning back to Jason.

Henry has never been one for big crowds of people or parties either. I wonder if he'll go. Part of me hopes he does, so he can catch a break from the weight of what this year has been and just have fun. However, the other part of me questions whether I'll be able to let loose and have fun meeting new people, knowing he is there.

'Why do you think you've turned down every guy that has ever remotely been interested in you, or always found something wrong with them? I'll tell you what's wrong with them. They're not Henry... and deep down you know he's the one you really want.'

My mind thinks back to Clara's words from last night, and I feel my heart sink. I can't go there. I won't. That door is bolted shut. I'll go to this party. I'll meet new people. I'll have fun, and I won't let the real world in. It doesn't belong here on this beach. August will continue to be my break from reality, even if it means a break from Henry, since recently it seems reality keeps hitting us both head-on, and pushing us farther away from how things once were.

8

Chapter Eight

* * *

It's just after 11:00 p.m. and all the *adults* have been asleep for close to an hour. They can never stay up late anymore, unless there's a mean game of Old Maid going on. Which we somehow all find ways to get really competitive over. I'm the reigning champ. Three years ago, I won our Old Maid championship for the third year in a row, which meant that I got to watch everyone else jump into the pool fully clothed, yet again. As I finish curling my last remaining strand of naturally straight hair, I take a step back to assess myself in the mirror. A wave of nausea comes over me. I haven't been to a party since I was like sixteen, and I left early. I just never really cared for them. And now, here I am going to a stranger's beach house all dressed up as if I do this all the time. But I don't. I have been the loneliest I have ever felt this past year and a half, and I fear that I've forgotten how to socialize outside of my family and our little bubble on this stretch of the beach.

Hopefully, this will be good. I can't let myself become a hermit. I've got to live my life. *It's obvious that other people are going to live theirs regardless of me.*

"Ooohh, you look good!" Clara sings as she waltzes into the bathroom to apply her lip gloss. She looks like a supermodel as always. The difference in our styles comes out as the reflection showcases her beautiful yellow dress that cascades down and complements her already tanned skin. Her dark hair makes her look like Belle, and next to my blue ruffled dress and curled blonde hair with a black bow tying half of it up, I look like I could pass for Cinderella. My freckled skin is the only hint that I've gotten any sun, and I take pride in the fact that I don't have to fall into that trend to paint faux freckles on my face. I get the trend, and I'd probably do it if I had to. Finishing applying my lip gloss too, we both stand back and run our hands over our dresses, assessing the final looks.

"We look good," Clara says. I stare back at her in the mirror, admiring my confident and strong little sister.

"Yeah, we do," I turn to Clara and give her a hug. "I'm so glad that no matter what happens in this life, we'll always have each other."

Clara stiffens under my grip. Another difference between us. She hates the touchy-feely affection, and I simply cannot be deprived of it. I keep hugging her anyway, and she finally lets out a sigh and loosely wraps her hands around my back.

"Alright, I love you too." She says before quickly releasing her arms and grabbing my wrist, pulling me out of the bathroom. "Now come on, we have to go meet the guys. Tonight you're going to make friends. You're going to have fun, okay? I mean, how can you not when you're with me?" I roll my eyes, but smile widely as my little sister takes my hand and we head down to meet Henry and Jason at the pool.

* * *

When we get down to the spot where the pool meets our little bridge down to the beach, I see Jason and Henry waiting. Jason is looking at Clara like she's the only person on this beach right now, and I can tell Clara notices, but she quickly hides any show of recognizing it. Henry is looking out at the now-dark water, seemingly unaware of us approaching.

"You guys ready?" Clara asks, and as she does, Henry turns back towards us, his gaze automatically finding mine, and if I'm translating his eyes right, then he either thinks I look great, or there's something on my face. I stay fixed on his gaze as he noticeably swallows, his voice then cracking as he responds. "Yeah, um, let's go."

A new confidence stirs up within me, and I loop my arm through Clara's as we begin skipping towards the beach. She seems shocked at my sudden enthusiasm and boost in energy, but she doesn't question it as she skips along with me. We end up walking hand in hand as we start the ten-minute stride to where the other guys told Jason the house was. As we walk, the moonlight hits the water in the most perfect and beautiful way, making it look as if stars are dancing on top of the whitecaps as they form. I look behind me briefly, only to find Henry's eyes instantly meeting mine. Heat rises to my cheeks, and I turn away. I'm not sure what has been shifting between us. There's been a shift in our friendship because of the distance, but the distance has also made me notice him in a new way. He grew taller and stronger. He became a man in the past two years, and I missed it. Maybe I was meant to miss it. I can't figure out the thoughts in my brain about Henry Rolland this summer, and unless he shows me I can trust him with my friendship again, I'm not sure I'll ever be able to fully figure out how I feel about my so-called "best friend."

As I continue to contemplate this, all thoughts about Henry and anything else at all come to a complete stop, as do all of our steps simultaneously, while we all gape at the house before us. A three-story modernized beach house stands tall in front of us. Drake is blasting loudly from the rooftop, which has a visible infinity pool and hot tub directly overlooking the ocean. People are swimming, and laughter fills the air. Blown-up pink flamingos are in the pool, and I immediately think of Katy Perry and that she somehow must have visited this house before writing *Last Friday Night.* A boy screams as he slides down a huge twisty slide on his stomach into the pool. Twinkly lights illuminate the entire back patio, highlighting the perfectly placed Palm trees and Azaleas. There are porch swings and round hanging bed swings placed perfectly around the patio, and a gold statue in the middle of the pool that looks like an Angel playing a trumpet, water shooting out of it. We are all still frozen as we take it all in.

"Okay, this? This is insane." I say aloud.

"Um, yeah… let's go!" Clara starts running towards the house, and Jason immediately starts after her. Henry and I remain frozen, staring ahead, but then turn to look at each other, eyes meeting to communicate once again. His eyes seem to say *What have we gotten ourselves into?* And I know mine say the same. I gulp, suddenly nervous again, my confidence dissipating as I realize how out of my comfort zone this is. I can't seem to get one foot to step in front of the other. Feeling Henry's hand engulf mine, I instantly relax. But as his thumb slowly caresses my hand, my stomach flips.

"Let's go," he says, and we walk hand in hand into this Katy Perry music video. As we inch closer, I already hear Clara's scream, and I turn to see her going down the slide. I didn't even know she was wearing a bikini beneath her dress, which I can now see draped over a poolside chair that looks so comfortable it could be used as a bed.

Oh, how I wish her confidence could rub off on me more.

Henry and I weave our way through the crowd of people to make our way over to where the food is. Whatever is being served smells amazing.

The party-goers are not who I anticipated. At the first thought of a high school grad beach house party, I thought this would be full of people drinking and bodies dancing wildly, which has just never really been my scene. So, I'm surprised when I find a lot of adults dressed as if they're at a cocktail party. Everyone is dispersed into different groups surrounding the pool, and it looks as if most of the college-aged students are in the pool. There is a game of chicken and volleyball going on at opposite ends of the gigantic pool that takes up nearly the whole front patio.

I wonder what the upkeep for a pool that size is?

We continue to make our way to the sweet smell that's coming from the inside of the house. There is a fully open wall leading from the outside to the inside, and we pass a couple of middle-aged men wearing collared shirts and sipping bourbon as we walk towards the table that I can now see filled with pastries. *Yay! Sugar.* I look at Henry, fully expecting him to be grimacing. When I look up, his brows are creased, eyeing the table. He doesn't love eating sweets late at night. He says it throws off his sleep and gives him too big of a rush before he crashes, resulting in poor sleep quality, which he has always taken so seriously.

"I'm going to go find where the drinks are and grab some water. Need anything?" He asks me while I continue staring at the mini bundt cakes and the assortment of different cookies. He takes my silence as an answer and says, "Yeah. I'm going to get you some water."

I simply nod and walk over to the table. Something about being at the beach has always kicked my sweet tooth into gear. I grab one of the way-too-small plates and pile it high with a snickerdoodle and peanut butter cookie, and then also add a mini red velvet bundt cake. When I go to grab a fork, I also notice the chocolate-covered Oreo balls. I freeze. One won't hurt. I said I'd have fun and let loose tonight, right? Well, this is my version of that. I reach for the perfectly dipped white chocolate-covered one on top, and as I do, a hand collides with mine, causing the Oreo ball to roll off the mountain it was on and fall on top of the plate of cookies next to it.

"Oh shoot, my bad! I wasn't even looking, my eyes were just on the prize." A deep voice speaks up, and when I meet the eyes that belong to it, I immediately recognize them. Ocean blue eyes, dirty blonde hair, tan skin. *The real-life Ken doll.* It's the guy from the beach earlier. He seems to register who I am at the same time, and we're both stuck in a momentary trance before I finally speak up.

"Oh, yeah, sorry. There are so many good choices here, but I couldn't resist these. I'm a sucker for anything Oreo."

"Me too," he says with a smirk. "I'm Kyle. I invited you and your sister here on the beach earlier, right? I'm glad you could make it. It's my little brother's grad party, and I just wanted to do something big for him. None of us thought he'd make it." He laughs lightly, and I immediately want to say something to make him laugh again.

"Well, it's a nice party. Honestly, it's more sophisticated than I thought."

"Yeah, there's a lot of potential business partners here, too, that I invited. My brother, Max, isn't sure exactly what he wants to do next. So, I thought I'd invite some people here who can give him some solid advice and direction. Just kick-start some networking for him." I nod in response, suddenly aware of how nervous and unpracticed I am in socializing. Especially with really good-looking men who should be full-time models.

All of a sudden, a beat drops and loud music starts to play.

Kyle speaks up louder. "Oh yeah. I hired a band to play for the last couple of hours, but would you wanna go somewhere quieter? Keep talking? I could show you around?"

My nerves heighten, and just as they do, I notice Henry coming around the corner behind Kyle. Two drinks of water in hand. I could very easily decline and stick by Henry's side all night, doing absolutely nothing different and meeting no one new. Or, I could say yes and let this extremely attractive man show me around, and potentially make a new friend who wouldn't be so awful to look at. I think of what Clara would do, and before I can contemplate even more, my lips speak for me. "Yeah, sure!"

Kyle grins deeply and gestures with his hand ahead of him, waiting for me to walk forward. As I do, his hand meets the small of my back ever so briefly to guide me towards the stairs in the far back corner of the house. I feel the heat rise to my cheeks, and as we pass Henry, I share the quickest glance at him. He's frozen, two waters in hand, eyes piercing with a fire behind them.

"This way," Kyle says as he continues to guide me up the stairs. I shift my focus and start walking up, Kyle close behind, and as I take each step further up, I can feel the weight of the confusion and weirdness between Henry and me from the past couple of days dissipate.

It's time I try to get out of my comfort zone.

As Kyle opens a back door that leads up to a rooftop hot tub with no other soul in sight, I realize just how out of my comfort zone I am.

9

Chapter Nine

* * *

I swallow the lump in my throat as Kyle casually takes off his shirt and gets into the hot tub. He looks at me expectantly.

"I'll just stick my feet in," I say while walking towards the edge of the tub. There are stairs that lead up to it, meeting a walkway that wraps around the outer edges. I sit on the driest part, slide off my shoes, and stick my feet in. The water is piping hot. At first, it shocks my body, but then my legs get used to it, and I let out an audible sigh. I can only imagine how relaxing it feels to be fully submerged. I hear laughter below, and I peer over the edge to see Clara on Jason's shoulders in the pool three stories below. He flips her backwards, laughing as she comes up and splashes him. I've really never seen her like this before. I find myself searching for Henry, but he's nowhere to be found, and my wandering eyes are interrupted as I feel the water shift. Kyle has moved closer now, his knees resting on the ledge underwater, right where my feet dangle. His knee brushes over my feet, and he puts one hand on the edge of the tub to my right. I feel enclosed.

"So, Elena. What do you do?"

"I'm a writer," I reply in a small voice. Suddenly, I'm really nervous. I don't know how to talk to strangers anymore. Especially a stranger who is a six-foot-tall shirtless guy in a hot tub, looking like he's about to walk on a runway.

"Really?" He asks. "Where can I read your work?"

My brain is foggy, and the steam is causing a sweat to rise on my face. My makeup is surely coming off right now.

"Oh, well. I actually haven't written anything in about a year. So, I guess you could say I'm more of an aspiring writer. I have just been dealing with some personal stuff. What about you? What do you do?" I try to shift the conversation away from me. I can't even talk about my struggles writing with the one person I want to, so I'm definitely not about to open up to some random guy in a hot tub.

"Well, I studied engineering in school. Right now, I'm kind of on vacation. I'm trying to reassess my priorities, but I'm still working on some remote projects."

I nod, but say nothing. He inches closer.

"Hey, um, there's something…" His hand reaches out towards the side of my face, and I immediately feel claustrophobic and too hot. There's a dampness to my dress from the steam now, and I am way too overstimulated.

Is this anxiety? Nerves? I don't know, but as his hand is inching closer to the side of my face, instinct takes over. Before he can say anything else, I shoot up, only as I do so, my leg gets caught in between where his knees were perched underwater. So, as I try to hoist my leg up, it actually gets tangled in his position, perfectly for me to trip. Suddenly, my dress is no longer damp, but it's soaked. As is my hair, and I can already feel my mascara running when I come back up from the steaming hot water. He quickly helps me up.

"Oh my gosh, I'm so sorry Elena, I…"

"It's fine!" I interrupt. "I should go home and dry off, but thanks for the invite!" I say, probably sounding crazed as I'm trying to hold back tears.

I suck at socializing. And, what was he even trying to do?

I want to go back to my safe bubble of the beach house, dry off, and forget this ever happened. So much for getting out of my comfort zone. I tried, and I embarrassed myself. This is why I prefer to stay in my comfort zone. I mean, what's so wrong with that?

I'm running down the stairs, holding both arms as I am now freezing with the chill of the summer night air against my drenched dress. I'm fighting back tears of embarrassment, and when I get to the bottom of the stairs, Henry is standing exactly where I left him. He locks eyes with me, and the fire behind his eyes is replaced with worry.

"El? Are you okay? What happened?" A tear falls down my face.

"I'm gonna leave now. I just…it was an accident. Coming here was just a mistake. I'm ready to go home. You can stay." I turn to rush out, but his hand quickly engulfs mine again, just as it did when we got here. I pause.

"I'll walk you, okay? I'm ready to leave, too." He can tell that I'm not really wanting to talk about my embarrassment, but he's still here for me.

He always knows exactly what I need. But I needed him so badly this past year, and he wasn't there. I thought he'd need me, too.

Another tear escapes, and he wipes it with his thumb.

"Come on, Cinderelena. It's past midnight. Let's get you home."

A small laugh escapes my lips at the horribly cheesy use of my name. I know his goal was to make me laugh. And it worked. He leads me through the crowd of people and walks us over to Jason, who is sitting on the poolside chair now, watching as Clara swims laps.

"Hey man, I'm gonna walk El home. You make sure Clara gets home safe, okay?"

Jason looks at me, and his eyes widen a little, but then they meet Henry's again, and he nods in a way that makes it seem as if he's just said yes to a very important mission. I know he'll get Clara home safe, and I know Clara feels that way too. Clara is underwater as we make our way out and down to the beach to begin the walk back. I'll have to answer her many questions later, I'm sure.

As Henry and I make our way to the edge of the ocean, he's still holding my hand, and with his other, he holds my shoes. We say nothing. I don't want to talk, and I know he can tell. He doesn't push. He never did. Oftentimes, we would communicate with just our eyes, but there have also been moments where we knew what the other needed without looking at each other at all. And tonight, as the moonlight shines high above us, casting only enough light for us to see a few steps ahead and the whitecaps of the waves as they break, he knows what I need without seeing anything else but the sand illuminated ahead of us. I shudder as a gust of wind encircles us, and Henry stops suddenly, takes off his sweatshirt, and places it around my shoulders. It's perfectly oversized, and it smells like cinnamon, vanilla, and saffron. I inhale a deep breath as I adjust the sweatshirt to a position that wraps me with its warmth and the calming smell. His hand finds mine again, and we walk in silence until I see the white and blue roofs of both of our houses, side by side, and the weight on my shoulders instantly lifts. *My comfort zone.*

10

Chapter Ten

***

It's been about four days since the party, and my embarrassing moment has yet to be brought up again. Henry has also not left my side all week. It feels as if everything is going back to normal. Promises being kept. Traditions being had. One of my favorite traditions when Henry and I were in middle school was to watch movies every night on the living room floor. We always made bowls and bowls of popcorn mixed with M&M's. Clara was always in bed early because she was younger, so it was like our special thing we got to do because we were "older." Tonight will be night four of our movie marathons, and Jason and Clara have been joining us, making it all the more fun. Jason really does bring an extra dynamic to the group. He fits right in. I think Clara enjoys his company too, though she'll never admit it to anyone, let alone herself.

***

The bells chime as Henry holds the door open for Clara and me to walk into the ice cream shop yet again. He lets the door slam in Jason's face, causing them to break out into a fake fist fight as Jason walks through the door. Henry ducks while Jason makes a sound with his mouth as if he just barely missed him. I exchange a look with Clara, and we both seem to be thinking the same thing.

"Boys." She says mockingly and loud enough for them to hear. Jason looks up at her, amusement in his eyes.

"Oh, don't even get me started on girls," he says. Clara crosses her arms and walks back to stand next to him and debate. Henry moves up beside me.

"It's your turn to pick the movie for tonight."

"Oh, I know. I've got the best one picked out. A true classic," I say, still eyeing the ice cream.

"Care to enlighten me?" He asks.

"Nope," I say, emphasizing the *p,* and turning to him shortly, meeting his eyes. What I didn't realize was how close he was standing to me, and that he was bent down to meet me at eye level. His gaze is burning into mine, and I forget where I am for a second until the boy behind the counter speaks up.

"What will you two be having today?"

I'm still frozen, and Henry keeps his gaze on me as he says, "She'll take a scoop of chocolate." He releases me from his gaze, and I let out a breath I didn't know I was holding.

I'm so hyper-focused on licking the chocolate ice cream that is threatening to drip down my hand, that I don't even realize someone is in the way of the door until I open it. I hit the back of a tall guy in the midst of me kicking the door open. He stumbles forward.

"Oh, I'm so sorry! I wasn't even paying..." I freeze as the guy turns around. It's the guy from the party. Kyle. He looks good, and I am still frozen with chocolate ice cream dripping down my hand as it falls from the cone. One second exposed to this summer heat, and eating ice cream becomes a race to finish it before the sun melts it all away.

"I didn't see you," I say in a smaller voice, memories from the other night replaying in my mind. No need to add to the embarrassment.

"Sorry," I mutter again as I turn to walk towards the car. I'm walking super fast, until one foot lands completely wrong, ankle twisting as I fall to the ground. My ice cream flies forward and lands in front of me, melting instantly on the hot asphalt. I hear running footsteps, and I'm too embarrassed to look and see who it is. An arm lightly touches mine.

"Are you okay?" Kyle's voice gently asks. He helps lift me from the ground, and I stand up quickly. I try to avert from his eyes, but when I meet them, I can't help but get lost in them. He is really attractive, and I am only human. Besides, there's no way for me to embarrass myself further in front of this man. Kyle's hand moves close to my face, and I flinch before I realize he's wiping ice cream off the side of my cheek. I hear a bell chime as the ice cream shop doors open again. Henry's eyes wander around the patio looking for me, and then they meet mine. I can see his eyes darken from here, but he doesn't move. We're seemingly both frozen in place, anticipating what Kyle will do next as his hand moves off my cheek.

Kyle takes a step back. "I was hoping I'd run into you, but not in a way that leaves you hurt and running off again."

I muster up a laugh. "Yeah, well, first impressions, and now I second ones, I guess... I've just never really been good at them. I'm used to being alone."

Why did I just admit that? I want to get more chocolate ice cream, make it to the car in one piece, and have my movie night.

"Well, I wanted to apologize for the other night. I hope you know, I just wanted to talk to you away from the crowd and get to know you more, but I could tell it made you a little uneasy. That wasn't my intention, really. I just think you're really beautiful, and it's kinda cute that you're clumsy. I probably didn't help by throwing you off in the hot tub either. I was just going to brush an eyelash off your cheek." I try to hide my further embarrassment as he says this.

"If you don't mind, I'd like to hang out with you again. You could pick what we do if that would make you feel better?"

I'm dumbfounded, and I make a quick glance back to where Henry still stands. His ice cream is now melting too, but I don't even think he notices. However, Clara is standing behind him, making widened eyes at me, wiggling her eyebrows. I laugh and look back at Kyle. He seems genuine, and honestly, why should I say no? I have no good reason to. I need to meet people. Henry's going to leave. Clara's going to college. There are three weeks left here, and I can't just run back to my comfort zone because I get scared of judgment when I embarrass myself, or for fear that change will just lead to disappointment. I've been lonely all year, and if Kyle had found me a few months back, I would've said yes to hanging out in an instant just to have some social interaction.

I think about what I would like to do with Kyle, as he said I can pick, and before I know what I'm doing, I speak up. "Actually, we're all having a movie night tonight. It's my turn to pick. Bring some popcorn to share, and you're welcome to join." Kyle smiles, and I feel heat rushing to my cheeks.

"I can do that," he says as a dimple deepens in his cheek. *Wow. He's pretty.*

We exchange numbers before he gets into his jeep and drives away. I walk back to the patio where Henry stands still, frozen.

Clara squeals. "Uh, what was that?" She giggles as I explain everything.

"Of course you fell down, typical El. It seemed to work for you, though," she laughs.

"Are you okay?" I look at Henry as he asks. His eyes say something new, but I'm struggling to read them. Concern mixed with hurt, maybe? Or anger? Why would he be angry?

"Yeah, I'm okay. Just need to get some more ice cream, then we can leave."

"Yay! Movie date night!" Clara sings.

"It's not a date!" I say.

Clara rolls her eyes, and I look to Henry one more time before going back into the shop, his face showing no expression.

What is going on in that mind of yours, Henry Rolland? And why does not being able to read you make me nervous?

* * *

Clara and I are just finishing up bringing more blankets and pillows downstairs. We decided on no living room floor bed this time since there's a newcomer. She grilled me on the whole interaction again as we gathered the pillows and popped the popcorn. She claims she's going to use tonight to get a good assessment of him, and that a guy's reaction to *How to Lose a Guy in 10 Days* says a lot. Kyle arrives just as Henry and Jason are coming in the back sliding doors. I go to let him in, leading him to the living room.

"You can choose your seat first since you're the guest," I say, gesturing to the couches.

"I'll sit next to wherever you want to sit," he says with that same dimpled grin as before. I turn to hide my blushing cheeks before choosing the edge of the couch that faces directly in front of the TV. I cover up with blankets as Kyle sits right next to me.

"So, what movie are we watching?" Kyle asks as he gets comfy, and Henry answers while tossing a bag of M&M's onto my lap.

"How To Lose a Guy in 10 Days." He says in a monotone voice. He grabs the remote, beginning to navigate to the movie. I look between him and the bag of M&M's that now sits in my lap.

"Thanks," I say.

He doesn't look at me as he mutters, "Mhm."

I look at Clara as she comes to sit next to me. She rolls her eyes, mouthing *"Men,"* and Jason goes to sit next to Henry, patting him on the back.

I decide to quit worrying about Henry for the moment and just enjoy my favorite movie. Although I am a little nervous with Kyle sitting right next to me. I pour the whole bag of M&M's into the bowl of popcorn as the movie starts.

Kyle leans close and whispers, "M&M's and popcorn?"

I lean in too. "Yeah. It's my favorite movie snack. Try some," I whisper.

He reaches in and grabs a handful before popping it into his mouth. He takes a second to assess before his eyebrows rise and he nods, approving. I giggle and then look at the movie, feeling Henry's gaze on me for a split second, followed by him sighing.

"I've got to use the restroom," he says before he gets up and leaves. He's gone for nearly half the movie, and only comes back when Andie is visiting Ben's family in Jersey.

Jason had moved next to Clara while Henry was gone, so now Henry sits alone on the couch. He doesn't say a thing, and I choose to ignore it for now.

The movie ends, and Henry immediately excuses himself to head back to his house and go to sleep. I let him be and offer to walk Kyle out to his Jeep.

"So, what did you think?" I ask. He looks at me with amusement in his eyes.

"I think that Ben was stupid to get mad at Andie when he was doing the exact same thing to her."

"I know, right! Ugh, but they are just perfect for each other! They were bound to end up together. Nothing could stand in the way of them working out in the end. I mean, when you look like Matthew McConaughey... c'mon."

Kyle laughs as I gush over my early 2000s celebrity crush. We get to his Jeep, and he pauses with his hand resting on the door handle before turning to fully face me.

"Thank you for inviting me. I had a good time. Really." His eyes are kind and genuine, the moonlight reflecting off the pools of blue. *So blue.* "Would it be okay if I take you out one night?"

I pretend to ponder it for a moment, bringing my hand to my chin as if thinking. He laughs. It's a great sound.

"Yes. I think that would be okay," I say with a genuine smile.

"Great. I'll text you," he says before leaning in and kissing me on the cheek.

I gush as he gets into his Jeep and drives away.

When I get back inside, Clara grabs my hand and yanks me upstairs before sitting on my bed with me. We spend the rest of the night talking about him kissing me on my cheek and what he might take me out to do on the date. I'm about to ask her about her thoughts on Henry's behavior, and even Jason's, when my phone chimes. We both see Kyle's name light up on my phone, and I open it to a text that says,

"Goodnight, Elena. I look forward to seeing you again."

Clara and I squeal, and I feel like I'm a teenager again. Carefree. The heaviness of my future not yet upon my shoulders. Kyle might be exactly what I needed this summer.

As I close my eyes to go to sleep once Clara and I finish crafting the perfect text back to Kyle, I can't help but wonder about Henry.

I wonder if he's mad at me, or if he simply just doesn't like Kyle. I wonder what happened between his playfulness when I ordered the ice cream and his sudden coldness when Kyle and I were talking in the parking lot. If I didn't know any better, I'd think he was acting jealous. But that's not Henry. That's not us. This past week has been great, just having my best friend back, and things are starting to feel normal, like past summers. But if he can shut me out so easily again, just like he did this past year, I don't even know what *us* means anymore.

11

Chapter Eleven

***

I'm getting ready for my date with Kyle, and Clara is helping curl my hair while I apply a little bit of lip gloss. We both look at the finished product in the mirror, and I let out a huge sigh.

"Why do I feel like I'm about to go to a high school dance or something? This feels weird. I should change." I run my fingers over the yellow sundress, and Clara grabs both of my hands at my sides before turning me around to face her.

"A man wants to take you out. On a date. An adult date. A real man who sought you out and has a real job and real money to pay for you. Make sure he pays for you," Clara says, pointing a finger at me.

I grab her finger and pull her hand down. "Okay." I sigh. "Okay. You're right. It's just been a while since I've done this. Like forever, actually."

"Believe me, I know. I'm shocked you even said yes. You always say no to guys in Colorado."

"Yeah, but guys in Colorado are… guys in Colorado. Kyle looks like a real-life Ken doll, and I'd believe him if he told me his job was *'beach'.*"

Clara laughs before enthusiastically agreeing. Kyle texts me that he's here just moments later. I told him not to come to the front door. Henry and Jason are downstairs hanging out, and Henry has yet to turn back to his normal self over the past couple of days. He's been short with me and oddly quiet. I honestly think it might be the looming decision of his internship getting closer. I'll need to talk to him more about that soon. I want to help him, and I also want to tell him more about this past year and how hard it's been for me. We keep pushing away reality. That's what we do in August. But I feel like reality is going to smack us in the face even more and make things weirder between us if we don't talk at all. It's been obvious he's in no mood for talking these days, though, and that's fine. I won't force him, but I also won't keep myself from enjoying my time here while I still have it. *I'm just not used to enjoying my time with anyone other than him and my family.*

* * *

Clara hypes me up as I leave before she goes to join Henry and Jason in the living room. Nana, Papa, and Jules are all out grocery shopping, so when I walk outside, the only car in the driveway is Kyle's blue Jeep. The doors and top are off, and I'm suddenly glad I have a hair tie on my wrist. Kyle gets out and walks around to the passenger door. He's styled his dirty blonde hair in a slightly messy yet put-together way. A few pieces fall to the front of his forehead. His Hawaiian shirt is unbuttoned a generous amount, and I definitely do not mind.

"Thank you," I say as I take his hand to help me step up into the Jeep. He goes around to his side and turns to me before anything else.

"You look beautiful."

I shy away for a second before meeting his ocean eyes. "You clean up pretty nice yourself," I say.

He nods, "Well, thank you. You ready?"

"For what exactly? Where are we going?"

He says nothing, but shows off that dimpled grin again, shaking his head as he starts his car and pulls out of the driveway. We turn onto the road, and I decide to let my hair blow freely in the wind, arms out to my sides as I breathe in the salty air and allow myself to fully let loose and enjoy this night. I feel freer as we drive along the road that follows the ocean, lined with Palm trees and colorful rooftops of houses. I look over at Kyle to see that he's smiling, admiring me in this state of mind, and my cheeks begin to hurt from smiling wider. I don't care where we're going. We could simply drive around like this all night, and it would be perfect.

We pull into Adventure Island, and the theme of feeling like I'm a teenager this summer again continues. There's a fake volcano surrounded by pirate ships where I can see a family cheering as someone gets a hole-in-one at the top. We're parked directly in front of a building with huge colorful block letters that say "ARCADE."

I turn to Kyle. "You should know before you commit to this that I'm really good at skeeball."

He laughs. "Yeah, I'll believe it when I see it."

He gets out and opens my door, taking my hand again to help me step down. When we get into the arcade, I'm shocked at how barren it is. Most families must have already headed home from vacation for school starting or something. I like that it's not so busy and overstimulating. I wander around as Kyle buys us some coins to use. The last time I was in any arcade, I was around eleven years old. It was my birthday party, and the first time Henry came up to Colorado. I remember he let me win every game since it was "my day." He got me my first fancy notebook and pen set, so I could write more. I still have it, tucked away in a drawer with memories and stories from when I was discovering my voice as a writer. Times were so much simpler back then. *I miss it.*

I'm broken away from my thoughts when Kyle's hand reaches around in front of me, showcasing a handle of coins.

I grab them forcefully and turn around. "Prepare to lose," I say, and skip over to skeeball.

We leave after about 2 hours of Kyle winning nearly every game we played. I almost beat him at the race car driving game, but one bad curve and I was done for. Still, he let me pick out a prize at the end. I went for cotton candy because it's been years since I've had it, and I have no idea when I will ever get to have it again. I don't find myself at places like this at home. I'd never had anyone to go with, and it'd be way too sad to be a grown adult alone at a Dave and Busters. Now back in the car, Kyle is driving to our next destination, picking pieces of my cotton candy for himself. I'm enjoying the scenery and looking out the window when the car behind us catches my attention. It's pretty far back, but it looks just like the Rolland's. *Surely it's not, right? That would be too much of a coincidence.*

I decide to let it go and just live in the moment. I'm probably just overthinking. This whole night is out of my comfort zone, but that's a good thing.

* * *

Kyle pulls into the movie theater. A place that Henry and I frequented a lot on rainy days when we were younger. We'd bike here in our ponchos before we could drive and buy one sour and one sweet candy to share. *When did we stop doing that?*

Kyle opens my door again, and we head inside. He orders us dinner and a movie. *Literally.* This movie theater has come a long way since I was younger. They now offer a full meal with your movie. We get burgers and a basket of fries to share. We get ticktes to watch a re-showing of Jumanji with Robin Williams, and I'm thankful he didn't pick a romance movie. That would be too awkward for a first date. I just want to have fun and laugh. Kyle starts leading the way to the theater when we pass a restroom.

"I'm gonna use the bathroom real quick, I'll just be a second," I say.

"Okay, I'll wait right outside the theater."

I nod as he heads the opposite way. Right as I walk into the bathroom, I see a flash of nearly black hair as a head turns fast, and a girl quickly locks herself in a stall as if she didn't want to be seen. I'm confused for a brief second before I see the shoes. Those black sandals from Target. That blue ankle bracelet with the seashell charm.

"Clara Martin!" I whisper yell. The door to the stall unlocks slowly, and Clara walks out with her head down as if she's a little kid who's just been caught stealing cookies from the cookie jar.

"What in the world are you doing here?" I ask, still whisper-yelling.

"Well, I was just too excited and curious as to what you and Kyle were going to do, and I wanted to make extra sure you were safe, you know, so…Jason and I may or may not have been trailing you and Kyle on your date."

I slap my palm to my forehead and sigh. "The Rolland's car. That was you guys?"

Clara huffs, placing her hands on her hips. "Ugh, I told Jason he was driving way too close." There's silence as I just stare at her. "I'm sorry, okay? I just wanted to keep my distance but save you from having to fill in all the details later!"

I shake my head and let out a laugh. This is so typical of Clara, and as long as she and Jason keep their distance, I don't even care. Tonight has been so fun. Nothing can ruin that. I'm honestly shocked she's here hanging out with Jason alone. Their trailing of our date… kinda makes them have a date of their own.

"Well, since you're so curious…it's going great. I'm having fun. I feel like a teenager again."

Clara jumps up and down, clapping. I quickly interrupt her celebration.

"*But*! He's probably going to come looking for me if I take super long, so just keep your distance, tell Jason to drive slower, and I'll fill you in on the rest at home, okay?"

"Eeek! Okay!" She surprisingly hugs me and then skips out of the restroom. As I watch her go, I'm suddenly aware of how Henry wasn't with them, and he was most likely all alone.

* * *

The movie was fun, and Kyle held my hand some throughout it. We're now pulling into the driveway of my house. He helps me out again, while also handing me the leftover candy to keep. He didn't eat a single bite of the candy the whole time. Henry and I usually finished it before the movie even started. But then again, we were actually kids then.

Kyle walks me up the steps to my front porch, his hand placed lightly on the small of my back. When we get to the door, we turn to face each other.

"I had a great time," I say, and I mean it. I don't know how I feel about Kyle. I mean, he's definitely attractive, but tonight was really fun because I was able to escape from the stressors of adulting and unemployment and just have fun like I used to be able to. I don't miss high school, that's for sure, but I definitely miss the naivety of being a teen in the summer at the beach. *2016*. There was something magical about that summer.

"I had a good time too. Thanks for coming. Maybe we can do something again soon? How much longer are you here for?"

"A little under three more weeks," I say.

He nods, and I slightly panic as he starts to lean in, but he brushes a brief kiss onto my cheek again before pulling back.

"Goodnight, Elena."

"Goodnight, Kyle," I giggle.

He walks back towards his Jeep, and I let out a breath before heading back inside. When I open the door, I notice the living room lamp is still on. Nana must have stayed up late reading again. I walk towards the living room, ready to tell her goodnight.

"Hey, I didn't think you'd still be.."

I stop dead in my tracks. Henry is sitting in the corner, his guitar leaning against the side of the chair. He has a notebook and pen in his hand, with his glasses on.

They look like a newer pair.

He looks up at me through them, and I can't read the expression behind his eyes as he asks, "How was your *date?*"

12

Chapter Twelve

* * *

I'm frozen, standing in the entryway to the living room. Henry is waiting for me to respond, slightly rocking in the chair. I really do feel like a teenager even more now, as if I'm being interrogated after coming home late from a date, except Henry is the one questioning instead of my parents.

"Um, it was good. Dinner. Movie. Typical first date stuff." I pause, but he just nods. "Why are you still over here? It's late."

"I got into a good writing groove, and I didn't want to disrupt the flow, so I just stayed put." He looks at his phone. "Oh, I didn't realize it was nearly midnight. So the date went well, then. You two stayed out pretty late. Why is that?"

He's looking at me as if he's waiting for me to tell him I fell in love with Kyle and we're going to get married. I'm too tired to deal with this conversation. Henry has been hot and then cold to me, and now he's acting overprotective.

"We played a lot of games at the arcade, saw a late movie. Nothing crazy." My voice is sharp as I respond.

"The arcade, huh? Did he let you win?"

"Yeah."

"Good."

Silence. Nothing but silence.

"Well, I'm really tired. I'll head back now. See ya around."

With that, Henry grabs his guitar and heads towards the back door.

I suddenly speak my thoughts involuntarily. "Remember when we'd bike to the movies in the pouring rain and share candy until we were almost sick?"

He stops walking, but he doesn't turn around as he whispers, "Yeah. I remember."

"When did we stop doing that?" He still doesn't look at me. "Henry."

All at once, he turns his head, and his expression is sorrowful. It looks like he's holding on to a lot of unsaid things, too. I want us to be normal. Best friends. He's always been so constant in my life. I don't want that to change because we both had difficult years and dealt with them poorly.

"I miss you, Henry. Don't shut me out. For whatever reason, you are... just don't. Please." He closes his eyes for a brief second, and then all of a sudden, he's walking towards me in big strides. His eyes brim with the slightest welling of tears, and it seems as if he's straining to hold them back from falling. I walk towards him quickly to meet him, taking his guitar from his hands and setting it on the couch before wrapping my arms around his neck.

I don't remember the last time we hugged, but as his arms wrap tightly around my waist and he lets out a shaky breath, I realize it's been too long. I needed this hug so badly on my loneliest days this past year. When I felt that no one understood me. I know he must have needed this hug, too; the last one we had was at Grandpa Joe's funeral.

Henry lets out silent sobs as I rub circles into his back.

"I'm sorry, El. This year really screwed me up. I miss him."

A flash of Grandpa Joe's smile plays into my mind as Henry says this. Joe really was the heart and soul of this place. He'd hate to see us so distraught over the unfairness that is life sometimes.

"Life isn't always fair, but as long as you keep those you call family close, you'll always have a shoulder to lean on and help you carry the burdens that may come." As I quote Grandpa Joe back to Henry, he lets out another shaky sob.

"Shhh. I'm here. I'm not going anywhere."

His arms grip tighter around me, and I feel my stomach sink at the contact.

"Thank you, El."

I'm not sure how long we stayed there wrapped in each other's arms, but as I go to bed later, I fall asleep thinking about how it felt. Henry's arms wrapped around me at the forefront of my mind. My date with Kyle already starting to seem like a distant memory.

* * *

The next morning is spent with quick runs to a coffee shop before heading out to the Tanger Outlets. Just us girls. This is a tradition that I look forward to every year. When I was in middle school, Nana took Clara and me here for the first time, and I felt like such a "big kid." The outlets stretch so far, all colorful and lined with Palm trees. I love outlets more than malls. I love how you can pop into store after store while still getting fresh air and feeling the warmth of the summer sun. We park next to an Academy Sports, and I think of Papa and Grandpa Joe. The only store they'd ever go in. I send a quick text to Henry before we start the mission to find cute clothes and burn a hole in our wallets.

Me: Have fun fishing!

Henry: Thanks. Night swim later?

Me: Absolutely.

Just as I'm about to put my phone back in my purse, it chimes again.

Kyle: When can I see you again?

I try to think of a response, but my mind is blank. I had a really great time last night, but something shifted when I got back and had that moment with Henry. It's as if Kyle has fallen low on my list of priorities, and continuing to mend things with my best friend has taken over my mind. I feel bad, but decide to forget about it for now. Today is for the girls. I zip my phone up in my purse, leaving it on silent. Hooking one arm through Clara's and the other through Nana's, as hers is linked to Jules', we set out on our way to try on more clothes and shoes that can fit in our closet. *I'm so glad I'm a girl.*

***

After hitting about eight stores and spending well over two hours in and out of dressing rooms, we decide to head to the food court for lunch. We pass a coffee shop on our way, and Clara rolls her eyes as I bolt inside.

"Addict!" She yells after me, but follows me inside with Nana and Jules laughing behind. "Yeah, well, there are worse things. Plus, we're on vacation."

Clara shakes her head, and I have no regrets as I order an iced caramel latte with oat milk. When the barista serves it, I am satisfied with the color. You can always tell if your latte is going to be good or not based on the color.

We all start walking towards the food court again, and I'm trying to decide on what I'm hungry for when Jules speaks up.

"So Elena? How was your outing with that boy yesterday?"

"Oh, it was good! We went to the arcade and a movie." I elbow Clara. "This girl and Jason trailed us the whole night, though!"

Nana starts to laugh while Jules' jaw drops.

"Oh, you girls are so silly. I would have been so mad if my sister followed me on a date with your Papa." Nana's eyes glisten as she says this. The memories of dating her high school sweetheart, rushing to the surface.

"Oh, I miss James. He used to take me on fun dates before he was away for work so much." As Jules says this, Clara and I share a look. Henry's dad has never been around. A workaholic at best. Henry only ever talked about him a handful of times in our letters throughout the years. Most of the times that he did, he'd only briefly mention fights they'd had about Henry's future. The mention of his name makes me wonder if things are still estranged between them since Grandpa Joe's funeral. I still haven't gotten a chance to ask Henry about the silent, yet heated argument I saw between the two of them outside the church that day. I asked in one of my letters, but it was among the many that went unanswered.

Clara senses the awkwardness and turns to Nana, arm looping back through her arm as she leans on her shoulder. "What did a date with Papa look like?" She asks.

Nana pats Clara's head. "Oh, we just had so much fun together. I remember one time, he took me to a drive-in movie. We had our first kiss there." She winks at us, and her smile is so bright as she recalls the memory. Eyes full of love.

"Oh my goodness! That is like something out of a movie."

"That's what it felt like. Dating your best friend is fun."

As she says this, Henry comes to my mind again, and I find myself imagining what a date with my best friend would look like.

"What are you thinking about?" Clara asks, and I realize I must have been in a trance. I'm thankful that we're now walking into the food court.

"Just trying to figure out what I want to eat for lunch."

As I wait in line at Chick-fil-A, I can't help but think back to my date with Kyle, and how different it would have been with Henry.

* * *

When we get back into the car, I go to check my messages. None from Henry, but another from Kyle.

Kyle: Wanna come over for a night swim tonight?

"Oh my gosh, say yes!" Clara squeals as she reads the text over my shoulder.

"I already told Henry we could go night swimming."

"No. This boy is cute, and he likes you. Henry will be fine. You've had nearly over a week to night swim with him. It's not your fault he's been moping around."

I think of Henry's coming apart just last night. Our hug that lasted forever.

"But.."

Clara interrupts me. "Nope. No 'buts." Tell Kyle you'll be there at 8:00. If Henry really wants to hang out with you tonight, he can when you get back. It's summer, and you're meeting new people. Stay out late and just enjoy it, Elena. Henry will be fine. Jason and I will hang with him, and then you can join us when you get back."

I stare at my phone still.

"See? You've left the poor boy on read long enough. He's texted you *twice.* You've got to at least hang with him for a little bit."

I sigh. Clara's right. I have always dropped everything for Henry, no matter what. Ever since we were little, I'd choose his side. I'd change plans for him unknowingly, until Clara caught on and pointed it out. I didn't even realize I had been doing it for so long. Besides, Kyle and I did have fun last night. I can hang out with him for like an hour, and then hang out with Henry and everyone else after. I owe it to myself to get out of my comfort zone more and see what new promises this August can bring. I text Kyle back.

Me: Okay. I'll be there at like 8:00.

Kyle: Great, I'll walk down the beach to meet you halfway.

I quickly text Henry again too.

Me: Care for a late-night swim? I'll be back from Kyle's around 9:00ish."

Henry is typing for a solid three minutes before his response finally comes through.

Henry: Sure.

I sigh and show the phone to Clara.

"See? He's fine. He's a boy. Saying "sure" with a period at the end doesn't mean what it means when I text it to you. It's good. He's fine, and if he's all pouty, he'll have to hear it from me."

I laugh, but deep inside, I find myself wishing that Henry and I were going to go to our favorite little bookstore coffee shop, share thoughts on each other's writings, and live in our own little world for a while. That world that only lives in this little beach town just hasn't felt the same, and I wonder if it will at all within the time we have left.

13

Chapter Thirteen

* * *

I'm walking towards the beach as I begin making my way to the halfway point to meet Kyle. I looked for Henry at the pool before I left, but I didn't see him. As my bare feet meet the water, I take a second to appreciate how small the ocean makes all my problems seem. I let out a deep breath. The peacefulness that comes from the ocean is like no other.

"Penny for your thoughts?" I jump at the sudden voice, turning to meet Henry's eyes under the moonlight.

"You scared me."

"Sorry. I overheard Clara mention you were about to walk over there to meet... *him.*" There's a pause before he says "him."

"I just wanted to make sure you made it over there safely. I was going to walk with you." I'm stuck in Henry's eyes when my phone rings, and the light from the screen clashes with and interrupts the moonlight's perfect glow.

"Uh, one sec," I answer the phone and walk further into the water. "Hello?"

"Elena, hey. So sorry to do this last second. My brother's got some sort of food poisoning. I'm kind of caught up helping him tonight."

"Oh no! I'm sorry! That's okay, I hope he feels better."

"Thanks, yeah. I'm sure he'll be better by morning. If he is, maybe we can do something tomorrow? I'll text you after my morning run."

I turn to Henry, his face questioning what's happening. I hold up a finger to him, telling him to wait a second.

"Sure, yeah. Sounds good."

"Great. Okay, talk soon. Have a good night, Elena."

"Thanks, you too. I mean, have fun helping your brother."

He laughs. It's still a good sound. "Thanks. Bye."

"Bye."

I hang up and look over to Henry. I somehow wandered deeper into the water when on the phone, the water now up to right below my knees. "Kyle had to cancel. His brother's sick."

"Oh." As Henry says this, his voice gives no emotion, yet his eyes seem to show a sense of relief. I realize at this moment, I'm glad to be spending time with Henry instead. I think back to Kyle's laugh on the phone just now. He had a great laugh, but so did Henry. I just haven't heard it in so long. All of a sudden, I feel the strongest urge to hear that laugh. To bring a smile to Henry that would reach his eyes, the way they rarely have this August. An idea comes to mind, and I spend no time pondering whether or not to do it. I quickly grab my foot as if in pain, attempting to make it seem like I can barely stand.

"Ow! Ow! Oh my gosh, I think I just got stung by something, or bitten!"

Henry is immediately alert and runs into the water.

"Are you okay? Hold on!" When he gets to me, he takes my free hand.

"Hold on, let me see." He takes his phone out of his pocket to shine the flashlight. I think fast and grab his phone out of his hands before tossing it, along with mine, onto the dry sand. He watches me with a shocked and confused expression.

"What..."

Before he can finish, I push him into a wave that was forming behind him. He loses his balance in the current, falling backwards. The wave splashes over his head, and he immediately stands up at the cold impact. He shivers and then looks up at me through the wet, dark curls that now fall on his forehead. His shirt outlines every line of his chest. The moonlight is pouring into his eyes now, and I see joy behind them. But the look is immediately replaced with determination as he lunges for me. I squeal and try to run the few steps back to the sand, but his arms wrap around me quickly and tightly. The feeling taking me back to our long embrace last night. It takes my breath away for a moment, but I begin to laugh and shout as another wave forms before me. I'm trapped, waiting for impact as his arms hold me tighter.

"Nooo!" I begin kicking, and as the wave breaks, he doesn't let me go. I get drenched, and we both go underwater fully for a brief second. His arms hold me tighter again. When we emerge, I gasp and quickly turn around in his grip. His head is bent back, and he laughs. He genuinely laughs, his arms still hanging loosely around me.

"I missed that sound."

My inner thoughts come pouring out. His laughter subsides as he stares at me so intently with a smile that reaches his eyes, but then his smile falters as he looks into my eyes more. He's looking at me with that expression I can't fully read again. I suddenly realize how close we are. My arms are wrapped around his neck, his still clasped together at the small of my back, our legs slightly intertwined every few seconds as we try to keep balance with the ever-moving waves.

"El..."

"Woo Hoooo!" Splashes and shouts interrupt whatever Henry was about to say, and we instinctively spring apart. Clara and Jason are running into the ocean to join us. I look back at Henry, and that intense gaze is still there until Jason's arms wrap around his shoulders, and he pushes Henry under. Henry comes back up, splashing Jason as they begin wrestling. Clara wades over to me.

"What happened to Kyle?" Her tone is accusatory.

"His brother got sick." She eyes me suspiciously. "He did! Really! Kyle and I are going to do something tomorrow." She nods, seeming to be satisfied with that answer.

"Good."

We get splashed in the crossfire of Jason and Henry's ongoing battle and move back a little. "Don't think I didn't catch that little moment a second ago…" Clara whispers.

I freeze, and can't think of anything else to do or say in that moment. I splash her with water, and she shrieks.

"Elena!" I can tell she's trying to seem mad, but instead she laughs as she splashes me back.

"Uh oh! The girls wanna join the fight!" Jason yells as he picks up Clara and tosses her into a wave, and a water fight breaks out among us *adults*. Sometimes, the ocean brings peace. A calm serenity that cannot be achieved by anything but the sounds of waves breaking on the sand. Right now, it's filled with sounds of waves breaking and laughter echoing, and it's bringing me so much joy. The joy of feeling free. The joy of a child. This joy is something I wish I could bottle up and save for rainy days. As I look around for a brief second between splashes being targeted at me, I realize the joy is found in the people I'm with, and the ocean just enhances it.

I take a deep breath before Henry pushes me into the next wave.

14

Chapter Fourteen

* * *

The pool water was cold as my feet dangled in, swinging from front to back. I was trying to get comfortable with the temperature before jumping in when all of a sudden, Henry's voice shouted from behind me.

"Cannonball!" I braced myself for the impact, tucking my head into my knees as he jumped over me, landing in the water with a huge splash that got me accustomed to the water very quickly. Henry came up laughing, and I too started laughing and kicking my feet at him in the water as he shook his hair in my face on purpose.

"Henry!" He pulled himself out of the pool and took a seat next to me, both of our feet now kicking.

"Let me see the new color of your braces again," he said.

I was reluctant, but smiled at him anyway. "Purple and blue are such a cool combination. I think braces look cool!" He knew how I felt about them. I think I'd complained about having to get them in every single letter I wrote him this school year.

"I can't wait until I'm older, and I never have to wear them again," I said with a forceful kick into the water.

"When I'm older, I want to be a firefighter."

I looked at Henry as he said this, questioning him with my eyes. "I think it would be so cool. I've been watching a bunch of firefighter documentaries, and my teacher's dad used to be one. He's told us a lot of stories. I feel like it would be fun."

I nodded, accepting the new interest. I think he would make a good firefighter. He's always been really strong, and he likes to help people.

"I want to write books like the ones that I like to read," I said determinedly. I've always known this. My first-grade teacher told my mom I would be a writer one day.

"You can. I'll be the first one to buy your book as long as I'm in it."

"I'll make you the villain," I joked.

"No! Make me a firefighter who saves the main character's life before they fall in love or something cheesy like that. Just make me cool."

I giggled as I kicked my feet at his in the water. "We'll see...What about your writing? You always say you want to write songs like the ones you listen to."

Henry sighed.

"Yeah, well. I doubt I'll ever get my dad on board with that, so you may just have to write for the both of us."

Our eyes stayed locked for a moment. "I believe in you, Henry."

His eyes smiled. "I believe in you, too, El."

Before I could say anything else, Henry pushed me into the pool, and we stopped planning our futures and just enjoyed being kids.

* * *

I'm holding a picture of Henry and me sitting by the pool, our backs to the camera. Jules had taken the picture as Henry and I were talking about our dreams and aspirations. It's been taped to my mirror ever since then. *It was so much easier to dream about things back then. I remember that conversation like it was yesterday, and now I'm nearly twenty-six... and I feel as if I have nothing to show for that goal I had.*

My phone chimes, breaking me from my doubtful thoughts, and I'm thankful for the distraction. This past year has been a never-ending loop of thoughts forming more thoughts that have stunted me, making me stagnant in life. I pick up my phone to see a message from Kyle saying that his brother is still sick and asking for another rain-check. I'm not relieved that his brother is still sick, but I am relieved that I don't have to see Kyle today. I've woken up in a bit of a funk. Last night, something happened between Henry and me, or it almost did. I'm not sure how I feel about it, and I'm not even sure I want to figure it out. I need to figure out what I'm doing with my life more than anything.

I lightly brush my fingers on top of the picture again. *I feel like I've let that thirteen-year-old girl down.* There's a knock on the side of our open bedroom door. Clara had shockingly left this morning to go for a run, while I opted to sleep in some more. I wonder if Jason had prompted her to do that. Henry now stands leaning against the door frame, eyeing the picture I'm looking at.

"Wow. I remember that like it was yesterday," he says while walking over to stand next to me. We're both standing in the full body mirror, looking at our younger selves who dreamed big, only now our adult selves are the ones staring back in the reflection. Those two kids in that picture had no idea what life would throw at them.

I sigh. "If only she knew not to dream so big." I feel Henry's gaze fixated on me as I say this.

"Come on," he says as he begins grabbing my on-the-go beach bag and walking towards the door.

"What? Where?"

"We're going to get you out of this funk. Change into a swimsuit and something comfortable. I'll meet you outside in ten."

With that, he's out the door, and I do as he says without thinking twice.

* * *

Ten minutes later, Henry and I are getting into the car. I decided to wear my one-piece hot pink swimsuit with white Nike shorts and my white Crocs. Henry has a loose blue button-up fishing shirt with his black swimming trunks on. He's wearing his white hat backwards, and *it looks good*. We start to back out of the driveway, his arm flexed and reaching towards the backseat. Before I can even process this newfound attraction, he speaks up, and I shift my eyes forward quickly. "Okay. So, how do you feel about saying 'yes' to everything for the next twelve hours?"

"Um, what do you mean?"

"Exactly what I said. We're going to get you out of this funk and get you trying new things. I know this year has been hard. You need a hard reset, and to be honest, so do I. Today, we're going to say yes to things we wouldn't normally, and we're going to get out of our comfort zones, and you're going first."

I'm staring in awe at him. He has the biggest smile on his face, and I know I do too. *Get out of our comfort zones.* He always knows exactly what I need. He finds new ways to read my mind. Sometimes, he knows just what I need before I do. That's why we work. I hope we'll always work like this. I've experienced a glimpse of life without him, and it felt like a piece of me was missing. But here, on this beach, in this car, driving down all too familiar roads, it's hard to imagine that those months without him even happened.

"Okay, fine. What am I saying yes to first?"

"Oh, you'll see. The anticipation is part of the experience." He grins over at me, and I get butterflies. *Surely that's just because I'm nervous about what I might be saying yes to.* As I look over to him again, his one hand on the wheel and the other readjusting his hat, I'm suddenly not too sure.

After about a thirty-five-minute drive, I look up from my Kindle, my mind breaking away from Emily Henry's depictions of North Bear Shores, traveling back to reality. We pull into an all too familiar parking lot. Cars are parked everywhere with families and couples getting out, carrying backpacks, hiking gear, and some dressed just like Henry and me with nothing but a beach bag. We park where the edge of the lot meets the edge of the rock formation, and I immediately feel like I'm sixteen again.

* * *

Elena's 16th Birthday Celebration

"You ready for the next surprise?" Henry asked as I was still browsing books. It had been the best morning. Since Henry wasn't able to come to my sweet sixteen birthday party back in November, he had been talking up a huge surprise day together once we both came to the beach this August.

"Yes!" I exclaimed, excited. I went to put the books back, but Henry stopped me.

"Get whatever books you want."

I felt like I had just won the lottery. I picked out five books and sipped on my coffee next to Henry at the front counter as he paid. I wondered if this would be what it's like to have a boyfriend one day, except obviously not

Henry.

He handed me the bag of books. "Here you go! On to the next surprise."

We got into his car and started driving to wherever he had planned next.

"I liked that coffee shop. Books and coffee are like the best combination," I said.

"Yeah. We'll go back sometime this summer if you want," Henry said, and I smiled widely as I sipped the rest of my iced latte, my eyes on the road in anticipation of what was next.

Where we ended up was not on my list of guesses. I thought maybe the mall, a movie, bowling... but not this. I was staring down at the water far, far below. I watched as a girl, who looked to be about my age, did a front flip. It seemed as if she fell forever before she hit the water, went under, and then came back up laughing. The guy who was with her was still at the top of the rock formation with Henry and me. He was screaming and clapping for the girl before he yelled for her to look out, and he jumped in, joining her. How did they do that without thinking twice?

I gulped. Henry was standing next to me, watching everyone jump in with a much more excited expression on his face than I had.

"I looked up free things to do around here that could be fun and found this place. It was a little out of the way, but apparently all the locals love it here. I think we should use the ropes over there. Those look fun."

I looked over to see the ropes he was pointing at. A teenage boy was swinging far out over the bay before he let go and fell far out into the water. I gulped again. I hated heights. All heights. I hated Ferris wheels, roller coasters, and the thought of planes freaked me out to no end. How were they able to fly? I would never understand. Henry didn't know this, though. We never talked about it, and I only ever saw him in August. The topic of heights or irrational fears just never came up. I inched forward to look over the ledge again.

"You wanna go first?" He asked. I turned around to meet his gaze, and

with one look, his expression changed from excited to concerned.

"What's wrong? Are you feeling okay?"

"Um, I... uh." I looked over the edge again, then back to him. His expression then changed from concerned to understanding.

"You're afraid of heights, aren't you?"

I simply nodded, my right hand gripping my left arm.

"I can jump with you." He took my right hand into his from where it was gripping my other arm. He immediately paused as he noticed it trembling.

"Or we can go rent bikes?" I perked up at the idea instantly.

He laughed. "Okay, let's go." And without question or disappointment, he took my hand in his and led me back down the trail. He knew exactly what I needed, and I didn't have to say a word.

* * *

I'm still staring down at the water below the rocks. People left and right are jumping off and climbing back up as if on a rotation.

"Time to conquer your fears," Henry says, his hand grabbing mine. I look to him, and then back down to the water below. *I can do this. I can get out of my comfort zone. I can say yes.*

"Together?" He asks. I tighten my grip on his hand, nodding with my eyes not leaving the water.

"Yes."

"Okay," he says. "On the count of three. One..."

"Two..." I gulp.

"Three!"

15

Chapter Fifteen

* * *

Suddenly, Henry and I are in the air, hands intertwined, waiting for the impact of the water. My eyes are squeezed shut the whole way down, his hand gripping tighter before we are fully submerged under the water. I feel a rush of energy at the impact of how cold it is at first. His hands find my waist immediately under the waves, guiding me back to the surface. When we lock eyes after catching our breath and wiping at the water now dripping down our faces, there is pure amusement felt between us. Pure joy. Fun. *It was fun.*

"I can't believe I just did that!" I'm looking up from where we jumped, wishing the younger me could see me now.

"I told you it's not that bad," Henry says. His hands don't leave my waist, and I'm all too aware of how they seem to fit perfectly there.

"Wanna go again?" His eyes are almost twinkling.

"Mmm, actually… I think it's your turn to say yes to something."

"Oh, come on! One more time. I'll jump with you again."

His eyes resemble a little boy's. I know he has so many decisions looming over his head. So much pressure. I think he partly used this day of saying *yes*, not only to help me get out of my own head, but to give himself the chance to just be a kid again. A chance to have fun before reality hits with changes and the many decisions of adulthood. We are having fun. Just like we always used to.

"Okay, let's go."

* * *

After jumping a couple more times, I've worked up an appetite and thought of the perfect place to take Henry for his turn to try something new. I'm behind the wheel now, and he is guessing where I'm taking us. There are beach towels on both of our seats with the windows down in an attempt to dry off before we reach our destination.

"Man, I'm out of guesses. I was sure it was going to be like the reptile part of a zoo or something."

"Um, snakes? No."

"Then where...no" Henry's voice trails off as I pull into the parking lot of Haru Sushi. I found it on Google when Henry jumped into the water on his own at one point. I was starving, and thought this would be the perfect opportunity to finally get him to try my favorite food.

"You can't say no. Come on," I say, grinning as I unbuckle my seat belt. Henry pouts while getting out of the car, but when I look back at him as he follows me to the front door, I can see the glimmer of amusement behind his eyes. He was never good at hiding how he truly feels. His eyes always give him away. I guess maybe mine do too. Or, we might just be the only two people on earth who can read each other through brief glances the way that we do. *I never want to lose that.*

As we eat our ginger salad, Henry is pursuing the menu. "It can't be fried?"

"Nope. Must be real, raw, sushi." He actually pouts fully this time.

"Okay, what about this one?" He turns the menu around, pointing to my favorite take on the Philadelphia roll. Avocado, cream cheese, and smoked salmon.

"I will count that one." He takes the menu back, dark eyebrows furrowed, assessing it further. He sighs, turning the menu back over for the fifteenth time when the waiter comes over. "You two ready to order, or do you need a few more minutes?"

Henry just shrugs.

"We're ready," I say with a big smile. As I order, I can sense Henry smiling at me, too.

* * *

The perfectly placed sushi is sitting on a long white plate in front of Henry. He eyes my plate, which is essentially the same but with crab on top and yum yum sauce. He takes a deep breath before grabbing a fork, but I quickly place my hand over his. He freezes, eyes meeting mine quickly at the sudden contact. For a second, it seems that there's that new look I can't read behind his eyes, but it quickly changes to a look of confusion. I simply take his fork away and replace it with chopsticks. He's staring at me in disbelief as I pour him some soy sauce and yum yum sauce into a tray. I sit back, cross my arms, and watch him expectantly. Still frozen, eyes locked on mine, he speaks up. "I don't know how to use chopsticks."

"Want me to get you the training ones?" I act as if I'm about to wave down our waiter when his hand pushes my arm down. He doesn't remove his hand from atop my arm as he says, "Absolutely not."

We stare for a moment more, yet again, and then he focuses on the project at hand. My hands are clasped together, elbows on the table as I lean forward in anticipation. He struggles for a second before finally fitting a piece of sushi between the chopsticks. He dips it in the soy sauce and then a little bit into the yum yum. With the sushi brought halfway to his mouth, he pauses, looking at me. I realize I've inched closer to him across the table. Feeling my cheeks heating a little in embarrassment, I move myself back some as he laughs and shakes his head.

"I've got to think of something more challenging for you when it's your turn," he says, looking back at the sushi.

"Oh, you'll be thanking me in a few minutes. Come on, try it."

With a deep breath, shoulders going up and down dramatically, he finally pops the piece of sushi into his mouth… but that's it.

"Now chew it…" I say impatiently.

He starts chewing. Slow at first, but then I see *it* behind his eyes. He's definitely not trying to show his second-guessing, but for a moment, as his head tilts… I see a flicker of joy behind his eyes again. His brows are furrowed as he brings his fist up to his mouth. He makes an expression as if he's about to be sick.

"Oh, whatever! You like it! You so like it! I told you!"

He pauses again, fist still at his mouth, but his eyes fixed on me. My eyes are saying *you can't fool me,* and he knows he can't too. He doesn't say a word, but then immediately goes in for a second piece.

"I just need to get a better taste, you know? To really assess how I'm feeling," he excuses. I nod, finally picking up my own chopsticks and digging in.

"Mhm. Right."

Within ten minutes, both of our plates are cleared, and I'm gloating as I skip to the car.

"Okay, okay. It wasn't that bad, but it's hard not to like smoked salmon."

"I told you," I say again, getting into the passenger seat. It's just after 12:30 p.m. now, and as Henry drives, my hands are out the window, swaying in the summer wind. My mind replays the new look he's been giving me. The amusement behind his eyes that has lingered all day. *His hands on my waist.*

We pull into a movie theater, and I'm broken out of my daydreaming as I look at him, confused.

"The movies? I'm not scared of the movies. In fact, going here is extremely *in* my comfort zone."

He says nothing, but gets out of the car and walks over to my side. He opens my door, his hand extended.

"Follow me," he says.

As I take his hand, I think to myself that I'd actually follow him anywhere if he asked.

* * *

Nearly forty-five minutes later, my head is buried into Henry's shoulder for the fifth time. I didn't even fully catch the name of the movie we're currently watching. He wouldn't let me see the tickets, and he made me fill up our drinks and coat our popcorn with butter while he got them. All I know is it's a horror movie, and I *hate* horror movies. So much. When we were younger, there was a summer when Henry and I crept downstairs past our bedtime to secretly watch the movie we heard Grandpa Joe and Papa watching. It was some type of scary movie, and I screamed at a jump scare, causing us to get caught and sent back to bed. That was the summer that our beach house was getting remodeled for a couple of weeks, so I spent most of that August sleeping in the Rollands' guest bedroom, which is currently Jason's room. That night, I was so scared. I couldn't fall asleep. I remember sneaking into Henry's loft room and him sitting up in bed immediately. He didn't even have to ask what was wrong. Even at ten years old, he knew that I was scared, and I couldn't sleep. We spent the rest of the night reading together. He was on his bed, I on his gigantic bean bag. It was one of the first times I discovered that he was my safe place.

Now here we are, years later, and I'm clutching the armrests of my theater seat while he laughs in amusement, stuffing his face with popcorn.

"You can't close your eyes," he whispers. "That's cheating. That's not facing your fears at all." He looks over at me accusingly, and I roll my eyes as he directs his head towards the screen, indicating for me to pay attention.

I look towards the big white screen that showcases the creepy old house. The young girl is lurking around, trying to find out where the noise is coming from. I turn my head, squinting with one eye open because I feel a jump scare coming. The music changes, and it's darker. *Any second now. Don't jump.* I try to remind myself that it's just a movie, but honestly, it feels like a game. I'm never able to catch the plot with the number of times my eyes have been closed since the beginning. I'm too hyper-aware of bracing myself for the scary parts. It's like that one YouTube video where the car is driving on the endless, windy road, and it seems like everything is normal, until a scary image of a woman resembling an old witch shows up out of nowhere on the video, screaming.

I remember when a babysitter of mine showed me that video when I was little. I cried. When I told Henry, he laughed and immediately pulled it up to watch it with me to see my reaction. Even though I knew it was coming, I jumped and covered my eyes when that woman popped up on the video. That's how I feel right now. I know it's coming. The girl in the movie is being extremely stupid right now as she follows the noise to the attic. *Every scary movie is the same.* She opens the attic door, the music stops, and for a few minutes, nothing happens, until...

"Ahhh!" The girl in the movie screams, and I don't even fully see what happens as the music picks back up with a huge banging of drums, and something pulls the girl into the attic before she disappears. My head instinctively buries into Henry's again, and I feel his shoulder bouncing up and down. He is so amused by this. I'm about to playfully hit him on the chest and move back over to my seat, but suddenly, he rests his hand on top of my own that is gripping the armrest, and I don't dare to move for the rest of the movie.

* * *

It's now nearly 5:00 p.m. by the time we get out of the movie, and I'm back behind the driver's seat. After like the tenth jump scare, I started to distract myself by thinking about what I should make Henry say yes to next, and I thought of the perfect thing. I'm nearly silent the whole drive, just waiting to see his reaction to where I take us.

"It wasn't that bad! That movie wasn't really that scary. I could have chosen way worse," he says. I glare at him, and his joy-filled eyes meet mine again. As I pull into the parking lot of my chosen destination, I look over to see his eyes shift from joy to fear as he stares at what's right in front of us. The boardwalk slingshot. Henry may be fine with jumping off huge rock formations into the water... but amusement park rides? He hates those. He always says they're too sketchy and he doesn't trust them. He swore he'd never get on one... but now he can't say no.

"No." He looks at me, eyes pleading. I shake my head and open my door, before walking around to open his, fully knowing that if I didn't, he would not get out of the car.

"Sorry, can't say no," I say as I lean my head into his side of the car where he sits, pouting. I leave him there with the door left open and walk away to go by one ticket. If I were nicer, I'd do it with him… but not after he made me sit through that whole movie. That lasted nearly two hours. This might last two minutes. He'll be fine, and I'll take a video of him screaming to hold over him forever. I'm waiting in line with him as we watch each person go on the slingshot, the sounds of their screams disappearing as they're launched higher into the sky. Henry is looking up and assessing every working part of the ride.

"I saw a video last week that went viral. One of these carnival-type rides malfunctioned. The people were stuck for hours. If this one malfunctions, I have a feeling it'll be another story." He gulps. I pat him on the back, and the staff member motions for Henry to step up onto the platform.

"You'll be fine," I say. He's shooting daggers at me through his eyes as the staff guy straps him in.

"Smile!" I say, zooming my video in on him. He only continues to glare. A few seconds later, he's screaming louder than the girl from the scary movie as the slingshot shoots him into the air. He goes up so high that I have to zoom in as much as my phone will let me to capture his face. His eyes are squeezed shut, and I laugh at the sight. I continue to zoom in as he makes his way back down slowly. When he finally comes into full view, his hair is a mess, and he's actually laughing. He looks like a little kid. This whole day has felt like us being kids together again, and I've loved every second of it. After he gets unstrapped, he walks over to me, glancing back up into the air as if replaying it in his mind. "That was such a rush! Wow."

"You want to do it again?"

"No way. One more time, and I might pass out."

I laugh.

"No. I'm serious. I might need to pick something chill for your turn."

He does look a little pale, but that flicker of amusement still rests behind his golden brown eyes. The sun is just now starting to lower to that picture-perfect moment when it reflects off buildings and the water in a way that makes everything look as if it's coated in honey. His eyes look like a pool of honey right now. I'm lost in them, but then he places his hand on his head and sways a bit.

"Let's just sit for a second before we do anything else," I say. He laughs and lets me take his hand and lead us over to a bench nearby. A breeze hits us just as we sit, and I watch him close his eyes and let out a sigh.

"Have you thought up any ideas for your book yet this summer?" I'm taken aback as he asks this out of nowhere.

"How did you..."

"Your Nana asked me if I had heard any ideas for your book yet. She said you won't let anyone know what it's going to be about, and she thought I'd be the first one to."

I'm silent, taking in his question. I used to share everything I'd write with him. In every letter, I'd send and update with writings in the works, and I could hardly wait until I would get his letter back in the mail with red markings, praises, and suggestions. What he doesn't know is that my so-called "book idea" was just something I blurted out to my family to hide my shame and embarrassment of having no writing to show for myself or my "career." I didn't have Henry giving me encouragement in the months of silence. I didn't have any friends near me, as they all moved away and had their own jobs and lives to focus on. I became so trapped in and affected by my loneliness that it muted my passions. It's like all I could think about was the fact that everything was changing, and I didn't know how to deal with it.

Henry speaks up again when I'm silent for too long. "I know it's my fault that I haven't gotten to be a part of it. But, I'd like to be now… if you'll let me."

I look to the ground, suddenly feeling embarrassed. "I actually… don't have any ideas for my *book*. Honestly, it was kind of something I made up to make it seem like I was doing something important. How lame of me, right?"

"Oh. Well, if you ever decided to write a book, I think you could do it."

I shift my eyes upward, thinking back to the memory I had reflected on this morning. He believed in me from the very beginning. And, I know he believes in me now, even when I don't believe in myself.

"Thanks, but the last thing I wrote was the last letter I wrote to you. I don't have much inspiration in me. I haven't for a while."

Silence is followed by more silence, and then a simultaneous sigh as we both look forward ahead of us at the sunset that now turns the whole sky pink.

I keep my eyes fixed on the cotton candy clouds as I finally let my thoughts free.

"Henry, it really was the loneliest year of my life. Not only did you leave me in the dark, but all of my friends from back home moved away and really started their lives, while I stayed behind… and fell behind." My breath gets shaky. "And now? I have no idea what I'm even doing. You've got this internship. Clara's about to start college. And me? I'll just be where I've always been. Stuck. Not moving forward."

I feel his head turn towards me, but I stay watching the sun move lower in the sky. "You're not behind El. Even the people who look like they have it all figured out don't really. Every day is a new day to start again, fail again, learn again, and get better to try again the next day. That's life."

I finally make myself meet his eyes again. They're still golden, and the color has come back to his face now. His voice is low and soft when he speaks again, his eyes full of an expression that says he means what he's saying.

"I'm so sorry you've been lonely, and I'm especially sorry that I played a part in that. But I don't believe you're stuck. You just have to get out of your own head and realize your potential is there for all you want to achieve; you just have to believe it. Don't give up."

I nod with a big sigh. "Thanks."

I don't know what else to say, and I'm grateful when he doesn't push. He simply brings me in for a hug, and I feel every ounce of stress, sadness, and fear leave my body as I exhale into his embrace. After all this time, he's still my safe place.

"Okay," he says as we pull apart. Each of his hands rests on my shoulders. "I know exactly what you're going to say *yes to* next."

* * *

About forty-five minutes later, I wake up feeling the familiar turn into the driveway. I'd know the feeling of that turn no matter how deep I'd been sleeping. I stretch as Henry turns the car off, and when I look at him, he grins and lets out a laugh.

"What?" I ask, pulling down the mirror.

There's a mark on my cheek from where I'd been lying on the center console. I rub it, but the mark remains, still. He laughs again when I shut the mirror in frustration.

"Okay." I yawn. "What am I saying yes to?"

"Well, it requires some brain power. So, go eat some dinner, put on some comfy clothes, and then meet me in my room, okay?"

I nod. "Okay."

When I head inside to change and eat dinner, Clara is heading down the stairs.

"You good?" Clara asks when she passes me on the steps.

"Me? Uh, yeah. Yeah, just tired. I'm gonna change. I'll be down in a sec."

When I finally get to our room and shut the door behind me, I can't stop thinking about today, his hug, the feeling of his hands at my waist, and that I'll be meeting him in his room later. Tonight.

16

Chapter Sixteen

* * *

It's a little after 8:00 p.m. when we all finish eating dinner. Tonight was just Papa, Nana, Clara, and me. When I looked around the table as Clara teased Papa about his small-town country accent when he pronounced the word *pool*, and Nana chimed in laughing, I felt a weight lift off my chest. Henry was right. I'm not alone. I feel so lucky to have the family that I have, and this little slice of paradise that is our own. A promise that will never be broken.

As I slide on my sandals to head over to Henry's, Clara stops me at the door.

"Where are you going?"

"Henry's."

"Oh. Well, how's Kyle?" She wiggles her eyebrows and glares accusingly.

"Um, he's fine. I guess. I didn't see him today." I avoid her eyes.

In a sarcastic tone, she responds. *"Really?* That's strange. Jason and I also didn't see Henry all day. No matter where we looked… we couldn't find either of you."

I narrow my eyes at her and attempt to hide the smile that is forming under my scowl.

"Oh. You and *Jason* couldn't find us? So you spent the whole day with Jason then? How was that?"

She returns the smile beneath the scowl. "Okay. Not going there. Have fun with Henry," she says, quickly dismissing the topic, but I see the glimmer in her eyes as she skips back to the living room.

Right as I go to leave, I run into Jason walking up our back patio steps. I keep the door open and turn my head towards Clara. "Oh, well, hello Jason!"

Clara's eyes go wide as I say this dramatically, and she immediately jumps off the couch. I laugh as I walk out the door, leaving it open for Jason to come in. As I start walking down the sandy path leading to Henry's back patio, I shake my head, still laughing.

"What's got you smiling to yourself?" I look up at the sound of Henry's voice as I get to the steps that lead up to the deck.

"Oh. Jason obviously being into Clara. Clara thinking that she's not being obvious about the fact that she is also very much into him."

Henry laughs, and even though I've heard his laugh a million times today, I can't get over it. Something shifted between us this past year when we had so much distance.

I'm not sure if it's the cliche 'distance makes the heart grow fonder' or the summer heat… but my heart has most definitely grown fonder of Henry Rolland.

It beats faster as I follow him up the stairs to his loft.

* * *

It feels weird being in his loft again. Henry and I haven't spent any time up here alone since we were like twelve. There were a few years when Henry started high school that he had his first girlfriend, and things were weird between us for a minute there. I never met her, but I always felt uncomfortable spending one-on-one time with Henry during that time. After they broke up, we just never really hung out in his room for movies anymore. It also felt weirder as we got older. Now? It feels like I'm a teenager seeing my crush's bedroom for the first time. Only, it's Henry. I know him better than anyone, and I remember exactly what this room looks like.

As I walk in, memories of watching movies and reading stories late into the night come to mind. His loft looks as if it's been frozen in time. His full-size bed still has the same blue plaid comforter with matching pillows. The same floor lamp stands tall with warm light pouring from the corner of his room. His desk still faces the wall, just underneath the slanted skylight window. Next to his desk, in the corner, is my favorite part of his room. His gigantic navy blue bean bag that could easily be used as a bed lies there, ready for me to take back my spot. It was always my spot when we'd read in here for hours back in middle school. Next to the bean bag's corner is his bookshelf filled with textbooks from college when he used to study for summer classes, songwriting books, and all of the classics. I immediately eye *The Great Gatsby,* and walk towards it. As I pull it off the shelf and open the front page, I see my scribbled handwriting.

To Henry,

You'll never be as cool as Gatsby, but you can try.

-El

"That one's still your favorite? Even though it has the worst ending ever?" I feel Henry's breath as he asks this while standing right behind me.

He walked so silently, I didn't even realize he had followed me over to the shelf. I was stuck in the nostalgic feeling of this room, in a trance of past Augusts. I turn around to meet his eyes again. They're warm, a mix of milk and dark chocolate, as the dimmed lamp in the corner reflects into them. They're smiling.

He has one arm outstretched to lean his hand on the bookcase, his bicep extremely close to my face. I glance ever so quickly before meeting his gaze again. Something flickers in his eyes, a darkness added beneath the light and warm glance from just before.

"It's definitely a different vibe than *Beach Read,* but it will always be my favorite classic. I'll always imagine Leonardo DiCaprio when I read it, too, which makes it better."

He immediately removes his hand from next to me, and I let out a breath I didn't realize I was holding. His hand reaches his forehead, and he visibly cringes. "You fell victim to all of those trendy beach books that are all essentially the same thing?"

I immediately come to *Beach Read's* defense. "Hey, don't knock it till you try it. Besides, you remind me of Augustus in some ways, actually. Right now, especially."

"Is that so?" His gaze is warmer, yet darker.

"It is."

There's a tension between us that I've never felt before. I'm not sure if it's this room, if it's just me, or if he feels the shift between us this August, too. I don't know what to do about it, but for now, I can focus on why I'm here at this moment. I'll figure the rest out later, if there's even anything to figure out.

"Okay." I take one more deep breath, gathering myself. "What the heck am I saying *yes* to?"

Henry says nothing, but instead, he motions for me to follow him over to his desk. He slides out the chair for me and inclines for me to sit. So, I do. Henry's laptop is placed in the middle of his desk, and when he opens it for me, a lump forms in my throat. Staring back at me is a blank Word document. My eyes follow him as he then goes to his speaker and puts on an instrumental Taylor Swift playlist. It's all piano ballads. *My favorite.* He then walks back over to me, placing one hand on the back of the chair as he kneels down to reach my eye level.

"I know this year has been hard, and I know you've felt stuck. But I believe in you, El. Even when you don't believe in yourself, I'll always believe in you. I know you feel like you've been alone. I know you're scared to let people see inside that beautiful mind of yours, for fear of judgment. Of vulnerability. But right now, you're going to say *yes* to writing something. *Anything.* Just write from your heart until you can't write anymore. I'll be here next to you the whole time writing lyrics of my own. And then, if you're comfortable, we can share it with each other when we're done. Just like we used to. I want to be a safe place for you again."

His eyes glisten as he says this, and I feel a tear fall down my cheek. *He knows that he's my safe place. I do feel safe again. I feel like writing again.* Henry's thumb meets my cheek as he wipes the tear away, and I see his own eyes have become glossy too. We stay here just like this for a moment. I catch him as his gaze moves down towards my lips for a brief second before he suddenly springs up from his knees, now towering over me.

"I'm going to go make us some tea, get a bowl of M&Ms, and then we'll write until we can't anymore."

I watch as he heads downstairs, letting out a breath when he's gone. I turn to face his laptop on the desk. The cursor is blinking in the bare document that's opened, as if it's waiting for me to give it a purpose. For nearly a year, I have had moment after moment of staring at that cursor, pages remaining blank, lines unwritten. Even on the few days when I did feel like writing, it was as if I had nothing worth saying. But now? With the day Henry and I have had, getting out of our comfort zones and just remembering how to have fun like when we were kids,

I feel like I know exactly what to write about. I'm not sure where it will lead, but I do know where I want to start.

I don't think anyone else could have brought me out of my own head the way he did. *He always does.* It's like he has a direct line to the thoughts that invade my mind. As if he looks behind my eyes when his own meet mine, and he knows exactly what I'm thinking or feeling. He just gets me, sometimes better than I get myself.

I'm still staring at the blank page when I hear footsteps coming back up the stairs. Henry places a mug of steaming hot tea in front of me and then proceeds to put a bowl of M&M's and popcorn on the side of the desk. He then plops down on the giant bean bag that rests to the left of me on the floor. Setting his own mug of tea on the side of the desk, he launches his hand into the bowl of M&Ms and grabs a handful.

"Care to hand me my notebook and pen? It's just in the desk drawer."

I didn't realize how much I had been assessing his every move, that I jump a little when he asks. I open his desk drawer, and I swear I hear a small laugh under his breath. I grab his dark green notebook and black pen, handing them to him quickly. When he grabs the other end of the notebook, his eyes are pouring into mine yet again. My grip seems to be stuck holding the other end of the notebook, but when his eyes shift to look at it, I immediately tug my hand away.

"Um… the pen?"

I look at my other hand to see that I'm still holding his pen. I toss it to him, and it lands in his lap.

"You nervous or something?"

I am. But I don't know why, and I don't fully understand it. Am I nervous because I'm about to write from the heart for the first time in what feels like forever? Or am I nervous because I can't ignore how my heartbeat quickens when he looks at me in this dimly lit room?

"El?"

I look at him, sure that he's about to talk about the shift between us recently. *I'm not ready for that.*

"It's okay to be nervous. Just write whatever comes to your mind. Write from the heart. This is a safe place, and you're not alone. I believe in you."

Write from the heart, I think, as I let out a breath, both grateful for his encouragement, and the fact that he didn't catch on to the fact that he has a different effect on me now than he used to.

Our friendship has just gotten back to the way it used to always be. It's healed, and he's leaving soon. There's no point in risking that. Besides, I am not the most stable person when it comes to my emotions right now. I haven't been all year.

I smile and nod, and he does the same before we both grab our mugs to take a sip of our tea, set them down, and begin to stare at the blank pages before us that are waiting for us to turn them into words that tell a story, that paint a picture, *that come from the heart.* Before I even realize it, my heart takes the lead, commanding my fingers to press the keys, and I'm typing so fast, my mind can barely keep up with the words that are pouring out of my soul. It's as if they've been there all along, just trapped and waiting for the right thing… *or person,* to set them free.

17

Chapter Seventeen

* * *

"*Ohhh my gosh! Ahh! I can't believe it!*" I wake up to the sound of Jules screaming from downstairs. She sounds excited. I look around, remembering where I am. *Remembering everything from mine and Henry's day yesterday.* I'm lying on top of Henry's perfectly made bed. I look at his desk to see his laptop closed and charging. I had stayed up until nearly 12:00 a.m. writing. I couldn't stop. I haven't written like that in years, even when I was still frequently writing. I want to show it to Henry, but not until I'm ready. I still have more to say. More words that need to be set free. It's not complete yet. I look to the bean bag and see a decent indentation in it. He must have slept there all night.

"*Oh my goodness!*" Jules's voice rings from downstairs again. I make my way down, curious as to what's going on. It's nearly 11:30 in the morning. I'm wondering if Henry slept as late as I had. Yesterday was amazing, but it wore me out. As I make my way around the corner,

114

about to step into the living room, I halt to a stop at the rough and weathered voice that I hear.

"Come here, son."

I peek around the corner to see Henry's dad releasing Jules from his embrace and setting a hand on Henry's shoulder. He pulls him in for a brief hug with a firm pat on the back before he pushes Henry from him, keeping a grip on each shoulder as he looks him in the eyes. Mr. Rolland's back is to me, and Henry's hollowed and tired eyes meet mine for a second before focusing back to his dad's demanding stare. I haven't seen that look in Henry's eyes since he graduated from high school. I'll never forget that day, but I hoped that Henry would.

His dad smiled for a picture with Henry in his cap and gown, before turning to tell him that songwriting is no stable career, and that he'd be interning with him at the firm for the summer. His dad had sprung it on Henry as if it were a surprise. *A gift,* he had said. Henry was so unlike himself that whole summer before he finally told his dad at the end of the internship that he had forced him into that summer, that he was going to volunteer at a songwriting boot camp come the fall, while he took online courses for college. His dad was not supportive, to say the least.

Henry's eyes are the same as they were then when his dad told him, yet again, that his dreams were stupid. *Why is he here? He's never come here. August doesn't belong to him.*

"What are you doing here? This is so great!" I feel for Jules as she is obviously so excited. She loves her son, but she misses her husband. According to Henry, he's never been around but for weekends at a time.

"Well, I just got the most interesting call from a friend of mine in New York who has business with this songwriting boot-camp of sorts."

I gulp and hold my breath as I catch a slight glimpse of a passive-aggressive gaze in his father's eyes that shifts to Henry. He must feel so small. I do.

"He wanted to *congratulate* me on my son joining the group as an intern during this next year."

Henry is still frozen. Jules's eyes are pleading with James to let up on their son, but he also doesn't move. He just stands there, his back now fully facing me as I see the light continue to drain from Henry's eyes, hollowness left behind. *Please stop. Don't do this. Not here. Not in our safest space.*

"Of course, you could imagine my shock when I heard that you had already accepted this position. I had to act as if I knew about it, and now that I do… I figured I should come down and visit for a few days before my son prances off to *Broadway*."

Mr. Rolland's tone is accusatory, demeaning, and like nails scraping on a chalkboard. The more he talks, the more my head wants to explode at every condescending word. If he knew his son at all, he'd know that Henry's dream is not Broadway. He wants to write songs that people play on their commutes to work on Mondays, just to get in a better mood before starting their days. He wants to write songs that people add to playlists for road trips, allowing friends to bond with lyrics and notes that have been intentionally placed. He wants to write songs that could be considered a *rare* find when people discover them, only to lead to those same people forever claiming that they found the song first. He wants to do these things, and *he can*. He's so talented, and now someone has recognized his talent and offered him an open door. All his dad wants to do is slam it shut without even stepping inside to see what may be behind the door.

His head is turning back to Henry now. "What was it, uh… writing songs internship?"

"James." Jules's voice is stern. Her eyes have shifted from affection to a warning glare at her husband. Henry's eyes are still hollow. He says nothing. I can't stand to watch this any longer. I make my way around the corner, the floor creaking as I do.

Mr. Rolland turns around as I make my presence known. His dark eyes meet mine. He looks the same as he did the last time I saw him at the funeral, only his beard is trimmed more, and he's actually acknowledging me. I think he knew better not to do so at Grandpa Joe's funeral, knowing I had witnessed the whisper-filled fight between him and Henry that day, too. The same fight that occurred at graduation. The same fight that is brewing right now.

"Elena, darling. I should have assumed you'd be around here somewhere."

His tone is dry, but he walks over to pull me into a forced hug anyway. I now lock eyes with Henry's again over the shoulder of his father's embrace. I don't care that Jules sees me mouth the words, *let's get out of here.* She knows I won't put up with James Rolland, and I'll always help Henry escape his father any chance I get. Henry only nods, eyes still hollow. When I pull away from Mr. Rolland, I make my way over to stand next to Henry.

"Well, Elena. I'm glad you're here. Maybe you can help me…"

"Actually, I have to get going. I've got to wake Clara up. I promised her I would take her to coffee, and if I don't wake her up, she'll sleep the day away." I try my best to sound genuine. "Henry," I say. He looks to me with a flicker of hope beneath his tired eyes. "Can you walk me back over to the house? Papa wanted to take you fishing this morning, and it's already nearly lunchtime."

His lips twitch at the corner, and he lets out a sigh of relief. "Yeah, of course."

He takes my hand, and we say nothing as we make our way to the back door.

"Well, come back later, son! There's an opportunity I want to talk to you about!"

We hear the muffled voice of Jules starting to scold James again, before all we hear is the sound of the door slamming shut behind us and the calming waves of the ocean greeting us, finally. Henry lets go of my hand and begins walking to meet the water. I follow silently behind him, letting him have his moment. It's crazy how just yesterday, we were in our own world, revisiting childhood memories and feeling the pressures of the world slip away. Now, only half a night's worth of sleep later, reality has smacked us right in the face, interrupting what August is supposed to be. His dad doesn't belong here. He never has.

As we meet the water, we let our toes sink into the sand, staring out upon the big blue. *Henry saved me yesterday. He got me out of my head. He helped me write again. I won't let his dad ruin what little we have left of the summer. I'll save him too.*

"Henry?" He looks over to me, still looking tired, but his gaze softens as he meets mine. "I won't let him ruin our August. I promise."

He sighs and closes his eyes as he nods. Then, he takes my hand and we walk along the beach back towards my house, the salt air mixing with the heaviness that has formed in the atmosphere.

James Rolland is a force. Even out of sight, you can still feel his presence, looming over our tiny slice of paradise. *A hurricane threatening.* I just have to make sure we stay in the eye of the storm until it weakens. Until he leaves.

We quickly reach the slice of sand that is directly in front of my house. As we begin to walk up towards the back patio, I stop to let an oncoming runner pass us. When he gets closer, I begin to recognize him. *Oh shoot.*

He slows down as he approaches us, catching his breath when coming to a full stop. Henry is silent, but steps up to stand beside me rather than staying behind me where he had been.

"El! Hey!" Kyle's voice is genuine. Kind. I feel bad for blowing him off. "Hey Henry, what's up, bro?" Kyle does the typical boy handshake hug and pat on the back thing with Henry. I have to keep myself from laughing at Henry's confused expression afterwards.

He tries to hide it as he says, "Hey man. How's it going?" I see right through his facade.

"Good! Yeah, just going for a quick run before lunch." Kyle looks back over to me. "Say, are you free for lunch? I could pick you up! I'm just going to run back to the house and shower quickly first."

Kindness still fills his ocean blue eyes. I have no reason to say no other than the fact that I made up fake plans to get coffee with Clara.

"Actually, I already have lunch plans with my sister. We haven't hung out one-on-one much since we've been here. Rain-check?"

Kyle nods, understanding. "Of course. Just text me when you're free, yeah?"

I nod. "Yes, absolutely. I will." I smile, and he returns it.

"Great. Can't wait." He pats Henry on the back as he puts his right AirPod back in. "Good to see ya, man."

Henry just nods, and Kyle begins to jog away before turning around and running backwards for a brief second. "See ya, El." He winks before turning back around and picking up his pace.

I'll give it to him. He looks good. Running and whatever else he does are working for him. I look back at Henry, and he averts my gaze for a moment before we continue walking up to the house.

"So, did you write a lot last night? I fell asleep when you were still writing." He immediately changes the subject from anything having to do with Kyle or his dad's surprise visit, and I go with it.

"Yeah. I actually did. I emailed it to myself so I can finish writing on my own laptop."

He nods, and we continue walking. Our steps perfectly aligned. When we reach the steps of the patio, he stops abruptly.

"I'll let you go wake up Clara. Thanks for a fun day yesterday."

He's smiling, but it's not reaching his eyes. I suddenly notice how pale he looks. Almost sickly. "Henry, are you feeling okay?"

"I don't want to talk about my dad…"

"No. I mean…" I place my hand to his forehead and audibly gasp. Moving my hand to his cheek confirms what I thought.

"Henry, you have a fever. Come on."

"No, it's fine. It's probably just a physical reaction to the morning I've had, and I didn't really sleep too well last night."

I grab his hand and begin pulling him up the stairs and into the back door.

"Well, you won't get any rest you need in that house while your father is there. He thinks you're fishing, so let him keep thinking that."

He says nothing as I bring him into the living room and motion for him to sit on the couch. When he does, he lets out a sigh before proceeding to lie down. I go grab a pillow from the downstairs guest room. His eyes are closed, an arm resting over his head when I come back.

"Hey," I whisper, and his eyes flutter open. "Lift your head for me."

He does as I say, and I put the pillow underneath his head before he lies back down, eyes still closed. I look at him, wishing so badly I could take away all of his pain. I've never seen him sick before. There was one time when he got the flu in the winter when we were kids. His letters that he had written describing it sounded awful. I remember feeling so helpless. But seeing him here before me, lying down with no energy. Mentally and physically sick and exhausted…*my heart aches.* I place my hand on his forehead again. *Yeah. He definitely has a fever.*

I hear footsteps coming from the back bedroom. Nana walks through the kitchen and into the living room.

"Well, hey there, little lady." She walks around the couch, seeing Henry lying down. "Uh oh, is he sick?"

I move out of the way to let Nana's maternal instincts take over. She leans over, feels his forehead, and then clicks her tongue.

"Yep. Alright, young man. You just stay right there. I'm going to get you some medicine and a cold rag." I watch as she goes back to her room to get the necessities before Henry speaks up in a soft whisper.

"Go wake up, Clara. I don't want to get you sick."

"Henry.."

"*Go*. I'll be fine here with Dr. Nana. She's the best. I'll probably still be rotting here when you two get back." I laugh. His arm moves to rest over his eyes again.

"Okay. Text me if you need anything. Just stay here as long as you need, okay?"

He nods, but says nothing. I watch him for a few more moments before I hear Nana coming back in. As I begin to make my way upstairs, I hear Nana telling Henry that he's to rest here and let her know when he needs another rag or some soup. I smile to myself, thankful that I can share the blessing that is my family with him. I feel bad that he doesn't have that all the time. *His dad had better stay at their house. His own agenda doesn't care if Henry's sick or not, I'm sure.* He didn't come here for Henry and Jules. He came here for himself. To try and 'save Henry's doomed future'.

More like to save his own reputation, that's already fragile due to his own actions.

I bet he's already told all of his co-workers that Henry will join the office in the fall or something *absurd,* and now he's trying to save face. My mind is running a mile a minute with the frustration I feel. This is not how August is supposed to go, and I won't let Mr. Rolland ruin it. I promised Henry. I promised myself that nothing would ever disrupt this month. *This place.* It belongs to us, and Mr. Rolland does not belong here.

* * *

When I open the door to our room, I fully expect Clara to be asleep, but to my surprise, her bed is made up. I hear music coming from the bathroom and follow it to find that she's getting ready for the day.

"Hey, you have plans or something?" Clara jumps at the sound of my voice.

"Oh! You scared me. I was so in my element." All of her makeup and skincare is spread across the counter. She pauses her playlist, which I see is titled *"Getting Ready."*

"I can see that," I say with a laugh. "I was going to see if you wanted to get coffee."

"Oh, well, actually Jason offered to take me to get brunch."

I raise an eyebrow at her as she says this, but say nothing more, knowing she'll shut it down and might not even go if I do.

"Okay," I say. "Well, I need to talk to you at some point when you're free."

"I'll probably want ice cream tonight if you want to go later, just us?"

"Sure," I say. "But to warn you before then… Henry is currently downstairs sick on the couch, and James Rolland made a surprise visit and is currently right next door."

She immediately stops applying her mascara and faces me. "Ugh. Mr. Rolland is here? No wonder Henry is sick."

I laugh at her immediate disgust. We've never really been able to understand Mr. Rolland. All we know is that every encounter we've ever had with the man has not been a very pleasant one. "Oh, and I need to talk to you about yesterday. With Henry."

Clara gives me a side eye before finishing up her lashes. She begins throwing all of her makeup back into her bag on the counter.

"Oh, you mean where you two *disappeared* off to all day and into the night yesterday?" She says sarcastically. "I noticed you weren't here this morning. Looks as if your bed hasn't been slept in?" She gives me a side eye again.

"Okay. Okay. Don't get ahead of yourself. I fell asleep writing. He slept on his bean bag, and then when I woke up this morning, Mr. Rolland was there, and everything that happened yesterday feels so far away from where we're at now."

She turns to face me fully. She looks as if she might cry, her expression seeming to be full of awe.

"You *wrote* yesterday?" I forget that the only person who might know me better than Henry is my little sister. She was there through it all. She'd get home from school and make sure I was okay after having spent another day alone. She'd watch movies with me every Friday night since I had no friends to go see. She never pushed me when I said I didn't feel like writing, but always said, *You'll write again when the time is right.*

She walks over to me and pulls me into a hug without any hesitation.

"I always knew you'd write again," she says with emotion thick in her voice.

"When the time was right," I say, hugging her back tightly.

She pulls away, eyeing me with a suspicious and amused expression. "So, I guess the time was right with Henry Rolland, huh?" I push her away, and she laughs.

"Well, 100% on the ice cream later. I want to hear it *all*." I nod as she says this while she grabs her purse and slides on her shoes.

"Have fun!" I yell as she makes her way down the stairs.

"Yeah, yeah." She responds.

But I can tell by the way she skips steps on her way down the stairs that she's excited to see Jason, and my heart warms. As I make my way back into our room, I plop down on the bed. I realize now that I'm hungry and should probably eat. I also desperately need coffee as it is now approaching 12:30 p.m. I don't want to go into the kitchen and make a bunch of noise. Henry needs to sleep. I would go over and raid Jules's kitchen, but there's no way I'm going over there with Mr.

Rolland still there.

I think of Kyle and decide to text him now that I actually have no plans. I should explain why I've been blowing him off at the very least. I grab my phone and shoot him a text.

Me: Hey, turns out I'm free for brunch if you're still free?

He responds almost immediately.

Kyle: Yeah! I'll pick you up in 10?

Me: Sounds good!

Ten minutes later, I'm glancing back at Henry lying still on the couch. He's out cold, and I find myself wishing I could relive yesterday all over again every day for the remainder of this trip, but instead, I walk outside to meet Kyle as he stands with the passenger door already opened for me. I smile, but I know it doesn't reach my eyes.

18

Chapter Eighteen

* * *

I can't believe my eyes when Kyle pulls into the parking lot where we'll be having brunch. It's the library cafe where Henry and I used to spend hours writing and reading nearly every summer. It was our *special place*. I've never been here with anyone else but him. We haven't been here yet this August, with all the weirdness between us in the beginning, and now he's sick and James is here. I suddenly feel guilty being here without him… with someone else, while he's sick on the couch.

"I found this place on Google. Apparently, the locals love it. It's a quiet place, it's got books and stuff. Though you might like it, and it'd be a good place for us to talk."

Talk. Right. "Looks great," I say with a fake smile.

I don't want to tell him what this place means to me. It's mine and Henry's. No matter what happens the rest of August, and when Henry inevitably leaves and starts the next phase of his life like everyone else around me... I want this place not to change... *even if we do.*

Kyle opens the passenger door for me, and then the door to the cafe. A bell chimes as I walk in, and I'm immediately greeted by the smell of freshly baked pastries and espresso shots being pulled left and right. As I walk in further, the smell of books filling shelf after shelf just waiting to be read mixes in with the warmth of the aroma instantly. All of the best smells in the world are in this little cafe. I once heard that smell is your longest memory, and I believe it. This smell is so nostalgic, immediately bringing me back to memory after memory of Henry and me reading in silence for hours, getting coffee refills, sharing pastries, and writing as if we could write forever and ever in this little cafe. The more the atmosphere tugs at my heart and my memories, the more I wish I were here with Henry.

"You need a second to figure out what you want?" Kyle is considerate as he asks this, standing close next to me while his brows are furrowed, studying the menu that's hung up on the wall behind the counter.

Someone new today is working, and I'm grateful it's not someone who would recognize me. It didn't take long for Henry and me to become regulars, the baristas always knowing exactly what we'd want. Sometimes, they'd save one chocolate croissant for us in the back, knowing Henry and I would come and want to share one. I look for them in the glass pastry case. There's none left. I turn to Kyle.

"I'll just get an iced caramel latte with oat milk," I say. "I can get mine," I quickly add after, not wanting him to feel like he has to pay. Especially when I've been blowing him off, and all the while he's been treating me like a perfect gentleman would.

"Nonsense," he says.

Before I can object, he walks up to the counter and orders my drink, a cold brew for him, and then two brunch bowls for us both.

* * *

When we get our food, we both eat in silence, finishing our plates fast. I assume he'd been hungry from his run, whereas I have been too caught up in everything that's happened since I woke up, I had nearly forgotten to eat. When we both finish our bowls at nearly the same time, Kyle takes my plate with his to put them in the designated bin near the front counter. I sip on my coffee when he gets back, because I'm not sure what to say. My mind keeps wandering back to Henry, his dad, *and what I wrote last night.* Being in this cafe has me itching to continue writing, and the feeling is refreshing after not having felt it for so long.

"So," Kyle starts. "I wanted to let you know that I'll be leaving town for a couple of days. I've got a work trip I couldn't get out of, but I promised my brother I'd come back to spend the rest of the summer with him. His last summer before entering the *adult* world of college."

I nod. "How is your brother feeling?"

"Oh, he's good, yeah. We think it may have been some sort of bug that could be going around."

I think back to Henry, wondering if that's what he caught. Some island bug.

Kyle starts to talk about his work trip and what he'll be doing there. He mentions a really nice hotel he'll be staying at and something about a budget meeting he'll be leading, but I zone out as it begins to pour outside. He's still talking, but I don't hear a word he's saying. It's as if I'm looking straight through him. The sudden thunderstorm bringing me back in time to the last time I was here during a thunderstorm years ago...with Henry.

The forecast predicted rain all day, and we used it as an excuse to read and write for hours on end in our favorite place. We had biked here on our own early in the morning, and the time escaped us. Before we knew it, Nana, Papa, Grandpa Joe, and Jules had barged into the back of the library section of the cafe. Henry and I were both asleep on bean bags, books lying in our laps. We were so confused when we woke up. Neither of us remembered falling asleep. My head was so close to Henry's shoulder. I remember sitting up so fast, feeling awkward. We were only like eleven at the time.

A barista was standing with our family. Her eyes were kind as she said, "Your family called asking if you two were here. Be sure and let them know where you're going next time! I know those bean bags are comfy."

I remember how kind her eyes were because of how they contrasted with the daggers our families were sending down to us through their glares. Henry and I were banned from seeing each other for the rest of the day, and we had to both write apology letters to everyone, reading them aloud at dinner that next night. We hadn't known when they found us that they had all scoured the beach in the pouring rain, worried sick about us. Henry and I laughed about it every time it rained after that for the rest of that August.

"So, that's basically what I'll be doing, but as soon as I get back, I'd really like to take you out again."

I feel guilty as his question brings me back to the present day.

"Oh!" I say. "Um, maybe, yeah."

I feel so bad for not listening to him. I'm not even sure what he's said in the last few minutes, but I know he's going out of town on a work trip, and I don't want to turn him down right before that. He's a good guy, and he's been sweet to me. I had fun with him on our brief date, but that feels like a very distant memory. My day with Henry yesterday was the best day I've had in what feels like forever.

I wonder if it would be the best day both of us have had for the rest of the trip.

I have no real reason to shut Kyle out, and if I'm still not feeling it when he gets back, I'll tell him then. I just hate confrontation. I've never been good at it, and when you're used to spending as much time by yourself as I do, you start to forget how to even confront yourself with things, like how I never confronted my never-ending writer's block, or the fact that I had allowed my passion to remain stagnant for too long.

"We've had some unexpected company, so just reach out when you're back and we'll see," I say, trying to muster up a genuine smile.

Kyle seems a little disappointed, but quickly covers it with an actual, genuine smile of his own.

I just need Henry to get better, Mr. Rolland to leave, and then we can all enjoy what's left of August. Reality is not allowed to interrupt. Kyle says he'd call me when he gets back in town in a few days, and he spends the rest of brunch talking about a random podcast he was listening to on his run. Again, I hear nothing…my thoughts wandering to how Henry's feeling, and if his dad has come back around.

* * *

On the drive back to my house, all I think about is yesterday with Henry. How *free* I felt. How *safe*. The moments we stared into each other's eyes longer than usual. The moments when his hands lingered around my waist in the water. I think back to Clara's comments about Henry has been secretly pining for me. I think about how she pointed out the fact that I never dated. It's true. I haven't had more than a date with Kyle since high school. *Did I subconsciously do that because of Henry?*

I do remember one summer when he had his first girlfriend when we were in middle school. I remember getting awkward and changing the subject every time he ever mentioned her. If he were dating someone when he had been ignoring me all of those months, I think I might've fallen apart. I need to talk to Clara. It's almost as if I need *her* to tell *me* how I feel, because I can't admit to myself that *I might be falling for*

*my best friend... and that's uncharted territory for August. It's uncharted
territory for every month.*

I walk up to the front steps to my house, my thoughts still reeling,
when I hear Henry's voice boom through the door.

"I'm going, Dad, and you can't stop me!"

"Son, you're setting yourself up for even *more* failure!"

I can't stand to hear another word of this. I burst through the door,
heading straight to the living room. James and Henry's heads both
shoot in my direction as I stomp in. Henry is halfway sitting up, looking
as if he's been abruptly awoken. He still looks sick and tired. James
is hovering over him, but both of their eyes are fixed on my presence,
and I know they can feel the weight of my glare.

"I'm sorry, Elena dear. I came looking for Henry because we need to
discuss a few things. I found him being lazy, sleeping in your personal
space. He's just ignoring his responsibilities again, you know him.
We'll get out of your way."

"*No.* Henry will stay here. You will get out of *our* way," I respond
without a second thought.

I have never spoken to Mr.Rolland this way, though I have wanted
to. He takes a step back, seemingly shocked. I look at Henry to see that
there's amusement behind his heavy eyes. I know he's fighting a laugh,
also shocked by my outburst.

"Can you not see past your ego long enough to notice that your son
is clearly sick? He's not feeling good, he has a fever, and we invited
him to rest here and take care of him."

James blinks at me, and I continue. "I mean no disrespect to you,
sir, but you have never spent a summer with us here once. You have
barely written back Henry from any of the letters he's sent you over
the years when you've been away. You simply send a check with a
cheap card for every birthday. You *tainted* what was supposed to be

a day of celebration for him by crushing his dreams before he even attempted to achieve them. You couldn't keep from doing it again on a day that wasn't about you, but about laying Grandpa Joe to rest. About allowing everyone to grieve in peace."

His eyes move to the ground, seemingly in shame. *Good.*

I continue in the calmest voice I can achieve right now. "I'm sorry, but with all of that taken into consideration, you can't just expect to show up here and yell about your own agenda and opinions on his life."

I look at Henry, and the amusement has built within his gaze, but there's also something else in his eyes. The same look I've seen a few times this August, and the only one I still can't decipher.

"I.. I didn't…" Mr. Rolland is stuttering, so I speak up again to save us all from more of this conversation.

"Listen, Mr. Rolland. I'm sorry, but Henry needs to rest. He's going to rest here. You can talk to him when he's feeling better."

With that, Mr. Rolland nods and doesn't so much as look at Henry when he walks out the back door. I sigh and drop my purse to the ground as I plop on the edge of the couch next to Henry. I feel his hand reach up to lightly touch my arm. Looking back at him, there's so much behind his eyes. So much emotion, I still can't decipher it. He begins to open his mouth as if he's going to say something, when Nana makes her presence known.

"I've got you another cold rag, honey." Henry and I look at each other with a different gaze now. One that says, *I wonder if she heard all of that.*

"Here you go," Nana says as she places the freshly cold compressed cloth onto Henry's forehead. "Let's get your temperature again."

She places the thermometer in Henry's mouth, and I just stare. His eyes are closed, his left hand holding the rag firmly to his head. *He looks so miserable. I hate it. I wish I could switch places with him right now.*

As we wait for the thermometer to beep, Nana comments on what just happened. "By the way, good job, Ellie. I would have never called out Mr. Rolland on my own as another parent, because I feel it isn't my place… but goodness. That man always had something to say about how I spent my money, how I cooked my potatoes, how I baked my pies. I never said anything to him, but it always irked me. My pies are perfect. Your Papa thinks so."

The thermometer beeps, and when Nana takes it out to check it, Henry and I both let out a laugh, eyes locking again. He looks so exhausted, mentally and physically.

"100. It's going down slowly but surely. You rest up some more and stay here as long as you need, young man. We are your family, too."

Henry's eyes get glossy as Nana rubs his head, before she grabs her book and heads out to the back patio. I don't realize there's a tear running down my cheek until Henry's hand reaches up to wipe it, straining to reach it as he does so. When the tear is wiped away, his thumb caresses my cheek once more before he brings his hand to rest on top of mine as it sits on my knee. This is when I truly realize *I'm in trouble.*

19

Chapter Nineteen

* * *

A couple of hours have gone by since Mr. Rolland's visit. Clara texted me saying she'd be ready for an ice cream run in a few minutes. I decide to change into a sweatshirt and some comfortable shorts. Jason would be dropping Clara off any second, and I'll meet her outside. Being sure to make my steps light, I walk over to the living room to check on Henry one more time before leaving. As I approach, I see the now room-temperature rag has fallen off his forehead and rests on his shoulder. He's out cold, his chest rising slowly with each breath. As quiet and gentle as can be, I lightly grab the rag, take it into the kitchen to run it under some cold water, ring it out, and bring it back to where he lies on the couch.

I feel his forehead, and he doesn't so much as flinch. *I really hope he's sleeping this whole thing off.* I place the refreshed cloth on his head and take a step back, assessing him one more time. There's not much else I can do right now. His medicine is next to him on the coffee table. He has water, blankets, and pillows. I try to think of anything else he could possibly need when my phone chimes, and I read a text from Clara telling me she's out front. I look to Henry one more time, then to the back patio, where I see Nana reading her book through the window. She'll take care of him, and hopefully, after talking to Clara about everything, I'll be more clear-minded next time Henry is feeling better and we get a chance to talk. One more glance. Eyes still closed, chest rising. My phone rings. I turn from the living room as I answer it, headed towards the door.

"I'm coming!" I whisper to Clara through the phone, before hanging up and shutting the door behind me as quietly as I can.

* * *

As I finish explaining everything that Henry and I did yesterday, Clara pauses when I mention exactly how Henry had set up the writing station for me, and how he slept on the beach bag all night. Her strawberry ice cream starts to drip down her cone.

"Clara," I say as I frantically grab napkins.

She laughs. "Oh my, whoops." She begins to lick around her cone, ignoring the napkins I'd just placed in her lap.

"Okay," she continues. "So you mean to tell me that you blew off Kyle's texts and plan to friend-zone him, basically had the most intentional and fun date with your best friend yesterday, slept in his room regardless of where, and you finally realized I was right this whole time?"

"It wasn't a *date...*" I argue.

Clara gives me a look that says *it might as well have been.*

"Elena, I know I was always teasing you about Henry, and I did want you to get out of your comfort zone and just have fun hanging out with new people like Kyle, but… I'm officially team Henry now, and I think you need to tell him how you feel. You two would be…*epic.*

I scoff at her.

"Also," she adds. "Again, I really am so proud of you for writing again. I know I was super busy with senior year things right when you moved home. I'm sorry I wasn't there for you more. And, I know Henry wasn't either, but he definitely is making up for it…"

I nod and play around with my cup of chocolate ice cream, my spoon stirring to make it softer. Clara's head tilts down to meet my eyes.

"Ellie… you are blushing so hard right now." She laughs. I turn to the side, hiding my face. "I don't think I have ever seen you blush before, unless you count when you discovered One Direction when you were like twelve."

I turn to look at her, pretending to be all serious. "Harry Styles makes everyone blush."

"True," she says. I can see her waiting to tease me again, so I decide to turn the tables on her.

"Speaking of blushing…" As I say this, she gives me a warning glare… which I obviously ignore. "What's up with you and Jason, huh?"

Clara immediately finishes her ice cream, says "nuh uh, not going there," then gets up to throw it away.

I start to laugh, but I don't push. I know Clara, and I know if I push, she'll shut it down even for herself, and I don't want that. I think she and Jason could be really good together. If anything, I think they could be best friends and have something like Henry and I have. Although what we have has definitely shifted, and I'm still not sure how to handle it.

* * *

Back in the car, Clara brings up the difference between Henry and me again, not letting it go. "I really think you should tell him. You'll never know how he feels if you don't… but I would bet money he feels the same way. I would have bet money on it years ago."

I sigh and put my feet up on the dash. "I don't know Clara. I mean, we spent nearly a year not speaking, and that alone put a strain on our friendship. It just got back to normal. I can't imagine what pressures telling him would put on our friendship."

"That's true…but you also have to look at the circumstances, Ellie. He was dealing with trauma and grief, and when we're dealing with those things, we are not always ourselves. You know he's sorry, and you know he didn't intentionally do that to hurt you." Clara's going into college next year to study Psychology, and I know she'll be good at it because she's always tried to be my personal therapist.

"I'm just scared," I say.

"Well, some of the best gifts and adventures in life come from taking those risks you're scared of at first."

I sigh. I know she's right…and that scares me even more.

Before I can object again, she adds more. "Listen, Ellie. Growing up, I was always jealous of the bond you and Henry have."

I turn to give her my full attention as she suddenly admits this.

"But, as I got older, I realized that what you two have is what I want in a partner one day. I'd count myself lucky to find something like that… and you have it." I think of her and Jason, and what she may have with him.

"If you keep waiting until you think the time is right, you'll make excuse after excuse until one day… it's too late." She looks over at me from the driver's seat to make eye contact with me. "Don't wait on love, Elena. It's precious and it's timeless. Don't let it pass you by."

I nod, and am in awe at how wise my little sister has become. I don't ever want August to end, because it means she'll be moving away… *and so will Henry.* I really am running out of time. It could very well pass me by.

After getting back to the house, Clara immediately got a text from Jason asking her to come watch a movie with him at the house. She tells me briefly, and it takes everything in me not to tease her about it.

"Watch out for Mr. Rolland," I say as she leaves.

"Ugh, right."

She quietly leaves out the front, and I make my way to the living room to check on Henry. As I walk in, Nana is covering Henry with a blanket. His position has changed from earlier, but he's still out cold. I make eye contact with Nana, and she puts her finger to her lips, motioning for me to be quiet before also motioning for me to follow her to the back patio. I silently walk around the backside of the couch, pausing only briefly to look at Henry. His chest still rising and falling slowly. *I really hope he wakes up feeling better.*

* * *

Once outside, Nana pats the chair next to her. I sit down, and we both take a second to take in the sight before us. The sky looks like a painting with beautiful strokes of pink and orange. The sun is just beginning to set over the ocean. I take a mental picture. There is nothing quite like a sunset over the ocean that seems to take up the entire sky. The bright and warm colors contrast with pockets of blue above waves crashing. It is both the picture and the sound of *peace*. A flock of pelicans flies overhead in the perfect "V" formation, and I am in awe of creation.

"It never gets old, doesn't it?" Nana asks.

"Never," I say. "I don't want it to end."

I don't want August to end… because I don't know what comes after.

We appreciate the sound of the waves for a few moments more before I let my thoughts out freely. "Nana…how did you know Papa was the one?"

She smiles widely at this question, her eyes looking upward as if she can see the exact memory playing out before her.

"Well, your Papa was very popular in high school," she says, just as giddy as ever. "All the girls were interested in him, but I remember when we went on a special date. You remember me telling you about the one at the drive-in movie? Well, it sure felt like a movie." I smile, imagining my grandparents as teenagers.

"When we had our first kiss that night, I remember feeling like I could relive the whole evening forever and ever. I'd never get tired of the same movie playing, being in the same car night after night… so long as I got to be with him." She says this in a slight whisper, her eyes still looking upward, memories behind them.

I admire just how enthusiastic Nana seems as she's talking about it now. It's as if it just happened, and she's so excited to gush over her perfect date. *I want a love like that.*

"So that's when you knew?"

She thinks for a minute. "Well, Ellie… I guess I just kind of always knew. The more we hung out, the more dates we went on… the more I wanted it to never end. I wanted it *forever*." My heart melts. "And you know what?" She continues. "All the other girls at school wanted him too, but I didn't let it bother me because while they were chatting him up in the school hallways… I knew who he was seeing on the weekends."

She winks at me, and I laugh, tilting my head back. She clasps her hands together, bringing them to her chest as she looks up again, more memories held behind her eyes.

"Oh, and the day he called me from the Navy and told me to start making my wedding dress... Ellie. I was so excited I could hardly stand it. I was going to get to marry my best friend."

Marry my best friend.

My heart skips a beat at those words. "That's beautiful, Nana." She smiles wider, if that's even possible, still basking in the memory.

"I know you knew that part already, but that was just one of the happiest moments of my life," she adds. "Now... what's got you asking about finding *the one?*"

I feel my cheeks getting warmer. "I don't know how to even explain it," I say.

Nana gives me a knowing look. "Well," she says, raising an eyebrow. "I won't pry, but I will say, finding someone to love is one of the best gifts, and if you find it... you better hold on tight."

I sigh as I realize she's just said basically the exact same thing Clara said. Nana moves over to share my chair with me. She places a hand over my own before speaking up again.

"I think everything is going to work out for you, Elena. It's hard to be sure of things in life, but love is one of those things that will make itself known to you at the right time."

"Thank you, Nana."

She hugs me tight as I say this, and when we pull away, the sliding doors are opening.

"What are you two doing out here?" Papa asks with the brightest smile in his eyes. He always smiles with his eyes, and it's the most genuine look that I've ever been able to feel every time.

"Oh, just girl talk!" Nana says, all chipper as she pats my hand. She goes over, rubs Papa's back, and then retrieves her book from inside.

"Girl talk?" Papa says, teasing.

"Yes... why, do you want to join?"

"No!" He says with a laugh.

Nana laughs too, and I want to remember the sound of my grandparents' joy and laughter forever. What they have is special... and what Clara and I have with them is the cherry on top. One of the best promises that August brings is time with them, and I'll treasure it forever. Nana takes her seat and begins reading her book. I look inside to see that Henry is still fast asleep, so I grab *Beach Read,* and dive back in, ready to escape my complicated love life by reading about someone else's.

* * *

About an hour later, I wake up with my book opened face down on top of my chest. I sit up, groggy, as I don't remember falling asleep. It's fully dark now, the patio only lit up by the lanterns and bright moonlight. I look at the chair where Nana was, and I immediately sit up as I recognize who now sits there. Henry is rocking back and forth, a book that I can't quite see the title of in his hands. I start to fix my hair, having no idea how it looks after falling asleep.

I realize I never used to worry about my appearance with him before.

My seat creaks as I sit up further, and I mark my place in the book before setting it down. Henry looks up from his own book and over to me, a warm smile immediately reaching his eyes that look less tired now.

"Hey," he says.

"Hey... how are you feeling?"

"Much better," he says exasperated. "Nana coddled me and kept me medicated," he laughs. "I think I slept most of it off. It felt like one of those freak bugs that knock you down for a day."

"Those are usually short but so brutal," I say.

He nods. "Oh yeah, it was rough," he says with a laugh.

"But, you're feeling better now?" I ask, just needing to hear him say it one more time. He stares at me, his gaze intense under the moonlight. His dark brown eyes look nearly black, yet they're still warm and kind. *Genuine, like my Papa's.*

"Yes. I'm feeling much better, El."

Silence. Waves crashing.

"Thank you for letting me escape here," he adds. I know exactly who he means *from* when he says *escape.*

"Always," I say.

There's more silence, and we both look to the dark ocean. Waves glowing briefly before each crash to the shore.

"How was your day? I feel like I kinda skipped a whole day." Henry asks, breaking the silence. It wasn't an awkward silence, but peaceful. *Still.*

"It was alright. I went to coffee with Kyle, and then got ice cream with Clara." The silence begins to feel thicker at the mention of Kyle.

"Actually, we ended up at the Library Cafe… and the whole time I was there, I realized you and I haven't gone yet this summer."

Henry nods, his eyes still focused on the ocean. He seems to be deep in thought, and I'm about to speak up again when he says, "We'll go."

I feel nervous as he says this, but then he looks over at me with that same perfect smile, and I realize how much I missed seeing it in just one day.

"Good," I say, returning the smile, thankful that the night is hiding the blush that I feel rising to my cheeks now.

Henry draws out a breath. "I'd better get back to the house. I think I've avoided my dad for as long as I can. I need to just figure out how to deal with it now, so I can enjoy the rest of our last ten days here. Maybe he'll leave before then."

Ten days.

My heart drops at the realization. I've got a lot to sort out in ten days. "Okay. Text me if you need anything."

Henry nods with a small smile. The look in his eyes makes it seem as if he has more to say, but he just slowly rises out of the chair before walking down the back patio steps.

"Goodnight, El," he says, looking back.

"Goodnight, Henry," I say, my heart full.

As he walks farther down the path, I think of how badly I wish I could fight his battles for him. I think of how much I love how the moonlight reflected in his eyes, marking pools of dark honey. I think of how much I love his tanned skin and his dark hair when he lets it grow out. I think of how much I love being near him, and how easy it is to miss him even as he's just left. I think of how much I love him, and how much trouble I'm in… because there's no way out of this feeling.

This love.

It started and grew slowly, showing no signs of its existence before it snuck up. Finally revealing itself after it has taken over my entire heart. And now I don't know what I'm supposed to do with it. As I hear his back patio door close, I feel the distance making my heart grow fonder from just a house away… and I wonder if the same effect will happen once he moves to New York… *in ten days.* Distance may make the heart grow fonder, but right now I feel as if it's making my heart weaker.

20

Chapter Twenty

***

It's been two days since Henry went back to his house. I haven't seen or heard from him much, aside from one text that said, 'Talk soon.' I've been pouring myself into my writing ever since. Right now, I'm sitting on a towel in the warm sand, Papa reading the paper next to me. There's an umbrella that I'm slightly under so I don't burn, and I look over to my right to see Clara lying on her stomach, basking in the full strength of the sunlight. I toss a bottle of sunscreen at her, and she squeals as it lands on her stomach, breaking her from the trance she's been in.

"I don't need this," she says, tossing it back over to me. "I don't burn like *you*. The sun *loves* me," she says in a mocking tone.

"Fine," I say. "Have it your way. You may be tan now, but when we're older, I'm going to look like the younger sister."

She rolls her eyes at me, not having a care in the world. She's always been like that. Where I overthink, she doesn't. It's refreshing.

Sometimes I wish I could escape my own mind and see into hers.

"Clara!" Nana yells from behind, walking up to us from the house. "Are you ready for our walk?"

Clara perks up and puts her phone and AirPods into her beach bag. "Yeah, let me just go in the water really quickly!"

She runs for the water, and Nana follows her to where the waves start crashing onto the sand. A few moments later, they're walking away alongside the water, Nana's floppy beach hat moving ever so slightly in the breeze.

* * *

Papa is still engrossed in the paper next to me, and I take this peaceful moment as I grab my notebook and start jotting down writing ideas again. Henry's day of saying *yes* to things awoke something within me. When he sat me down, told me to get out of my head, and just write… it unlocked collections of words and images that I didn't know I had in me. Stories I didn't know I wanted to tell. Or even *could* tell. What I wrote that night was the most vulnerable thing I think I've ever written. The wall of writer's block I had been experiencing came crashing down, and it has not threatened to go back up since.

I sent what I wrote to myself from his laptop before deleting it when I was done. I want to show it to him, but now is not the time. I need to make sure it's exactly what I want to say. I need to make sure each word is placed perfectly. And, I need Mr. Rolland to finish his business and leave, so Henry can be in a good mindset for the rest of our time here. So we can have what's left of August… and so I can figure out what to do about my newfound unresolved feelings for my best friend. I guess I have my own business with Henry I need to tend to, but I've got to work it out with myself first.

The wind picks up, and it simultaneously blows Papa's paper out of his hands and shuts my flimsy notebook abruptly. Papa yelps and we both start laughing, scrambling to our feet and chasing his paper in the wind, winning some cheers and laughs from other beach goers. As we both grab the paper, it rips in half, and Papa blames me with a playful grin that starts in his eyes yet again. Henry may be my best friend, but Papa will always be my *best buddy.*

* * *

When just after lunchtime finally rolls around, Papa and I decide to go on a bike ride to the pier together. Another tradition, and one of my favorites. I remember the first time he took me there when I was little. I was so scared of when the people on the pier would bring a fish slopping around, over the ledge. I remember always having to close my eyes when walking past the table where they'd start to prep the fish. Now, Papa and I like to bike there and walk to the very edge of the pier and see who catches the biggest one. I haven't been back to the pier yet this summer since Henry's fishhook incident, but it's essential that I go with Papa. It's tradition.

I start to fold up my towel and stuff my sunglasses and sunscreen into my beach bag, but my head jerks up at the sound of that deep and demanding voice. I look up towards Henry's house, his dad coming out on the back porch, and Henry not far behind. Henry looks at me before he takes a seat next to his dad. Mr. Rolland seems to be having a serious conversation with his phone on speaker. My phone chimes, and when I look at it, it's a text from Henry.

Henry: He's making me sit in and listen to some of his business calls.

Me: You've got to be kidding me.

Henry: It's okay. He has to fly out to Jersey later tonight. If I sit through this, he'll be out of all of our hair in no time.
Me: Good luck.
Henry: Thanks.

* * *

About thirty minutes later, Papa and I are gliding on our bikes along the sidewalk that leads directly to the fishing pier. As we pass by houses, Papa and I play a game where we decide which houses each of our family members would be most likely to live in. We end up passing a small, beat-up, abandoned shack along a barren portion of sand.

"That one's yours!" Papa exclaims.

"Hey!" I yell back.

Papa is laughing in amusement as I speed up and pass him, taking the lead. For the rest of the bike ride, Papa talks about the many memories of Clara and me coming to the beach when we were really little, and my heart fills up with joy.

"I remember one year when you were still really little. You put your bathing suit on before we even started our long drive down here, and you refused to take it off." Papa's laughing, a twinkle in his eyes as always.

"I remember that. I was excited." I say, returning the laughter and reminiscing.

My mind is full of memories with my Nana, Papa, and Clara. It was just us for a while, until Henry and Grandpa Joe approached us on the beach that day. Grandpa Joe and Papa clicked instantly, and I eventually warmed up to Henry. Jules and Nana bonded over books in no time, and after that, we began to share August with the Rollands. It's hard to imagine August without them. I think of Henry and Grandpa Joe. He hasn't wanted to talk about him much this summer, and I can't blame him. Henry views August the way that I do. It's an escape from all the heavy things of life. We mentally drop our loads off at the Alabama state line and hope that when we cross back over it and August begins to end, everything feels a little lighter… the ocean having washed away all of our burdens and troubles.

Now, one of those heavy topics is here looming over us all. Mr. Rolland. I know if Grandpa Joe were here, he wouldn't have allowed James to storm in and demand Henry's time for dreams he didn't have. Hopefully, after tonight, Henry will be able to shake the weight off his shoulders and enjoy the rest of August. Hopefully, we can enjoy it together.

Papa whistles, breaking me from my thoughts. I hadn't realized we'd made it to the pier. We turn in, lock our bikes on the rack, and begin the walk to the edge, making bets on how big a fish we think people will be catching.

* * *

On our bike ride back to the house, it begins storming out of nowhere. Papa and I bike as fast as we can, and by the time we get to the house, we both drop the bikes and run inside. We are drenched as we shut the door behind us, water dripping onto the floor on either side of us. Our laughter echoes in the entryway, and Nana's jaw drops as she comes around the corner.

"Well, just look at you two! Stay right there while I go grab some towels!"

Papa and I look at each other as if we've just gotten in trouble, and Clara and Jason walk around the corner just in time to see Nana tossing us towels and demanding that we not track water into the house. As

147

Papa and I are drying off, and Clara is taking a video on her phone, I realize again how lucky I am to have the family I have. I realize how lucky I am to share what I have with Henry and now even Jason. And this is just a glimpse of the amazing family I have. I'm so lucky to have a loving mother and father waiting for me at home, too. I feel so lucky to be so loved by my family. It's a safe love that I never have to question.

I know Henry has that with Jules, but I don't know about his father. I quickly grab my phone, wiping the water off the screen to send a text to my parents saying I miss them. Then, I text Henry asking him if he'd be free after his dad left tonight. I want to tell him how I feel. I want to show him what a safe love feels like, the way my family has for me… and the way Henry has… all these years… without even knowing it.

* * *

The thunderstorm came and went quickly, but the waves it left in its wake look like the perfect waves for boogie boarding. Papa is the first to notice this, demanding that Clara, Jason, and I grab our boards and head to the beach with him. We don't hesitate, as waves like this don't come every day. I check my phone once before following everyone out. No text back from Henry. I sigh, leave my phone on the kitchen counter, and go to drown my thoughts in the ocean's waves.

Wave after wave comes, and Clara and I are almost tied for catching the biggest ones and being pushed the farthest to shore when we catch one. It's always a competition. She's just stolen a big wave from me, cutting me off, and I laugh when she flips over shortly after catching it. *Karma.* She comes back up from the water, her hair all in her face.

Jason swims up next to her, patting her on the back as she pushes the tangled strands away from her eyes.

"It was a nice try," Jason says, holding in laughter. I don't even try to hold in mine.

Clara glares at him, and then at me, before saying, "I blame Elena."

I laugh, and let her paddle after the next wave coming. I make my way out to where the waves are rising, but not yet curling over. I love to ride over them just before they break. It's like a mini roller coaster.

Papa paddles over next to me. "Let's wait for the biggest one and race, okay?"

"Okay, prepare to lose," I say.

After a few minutes have passed, we're still waiting, no waves seeming good enough to try and catch. I'm about to ask if we need to go closer to shore when a lady standing on a paddleboard loops around us.

"There's a Bull Shark a few feet away from y'all over there," she says as casually as ever, pointing right in front of us before paddling out further.

Papa and I look at each other with wide eyes before looking behind us to face the shore. I hadn't realized how far we had drifted as we waited for a good wave. The ocean can make your problems seem so much smaller, but it's also alive and has a mind of its own. A powerful one. It can become easy to drift too far when you fully let your guard down. Just like life. If you let your thoughts drift too far, or let your guard down too soon… you can get hurt. *I wonder if it's too soon to fully let my guard down and my feelings out with Henry. What if we hurt each other? What if our friendship isn't ready for that?*

"Alright, come on. Let's get back quickly, but also slowly," Papa says next to me as he starts to paddle, grabbing my board and starting to pull me along.

Clara and Jason are way ahead of us, riding smaller waves to shore next to each other. I begin to internally freak out, but I don't want to make sudden splashes. I suddenly feel like I don't know how to swim, not slowly and fast at the same time, at least. My mind keeps playing tricks on me with the movement of the current that's fighting to send us back out to the ocean as we swim against it. I feel like any second now I'm going to see a fin pop out of the water right next to me.

I focus on the shoreline, watching it get closer ever so slowly. That's when I see *him.* Henry is standing on the shore, his face looking right in my direction. I keep my focus on him. My breathing starts to calm down, and the strokes of my arms as I paddle become stronger, more controlled. The fear in me subsides the more I keep my focus on my best friend, waiting for me. With my Papa right behind me and Henry ahead of me, I feel safer than ever.

We finally get to where we can stand, and Papa and I quickly run out of the water, waves threatening to knock us over as they break. When I step onto the bank, Henry looks confused at the panicked look I know I'm portraying while catching my breath. I tell him what just happened, and he thinks it's cool, to which I roll my eyes.

"You say that now, but you wouldn't have thought that if you were the one out there."

He just laughs as I continue to catch my breath, and I notice the color is fully back to his face now.

"You look a lot better than the last time I saw you," I say. He rocks back on his heel, hands in his shorts pocket.

"Yeah, I feel a lot better," he pauses. "My dad left early."

"Oh," is all I can manage to say.

"Hey, I want to talk to you. Want to go to the Library Cafe?"

I gulp, suddenly nervous as he says this.

"Yeah," I say. "Let me just change. I'll meet you outside in twenty?"

"Sounds great," he says, and I feel like I'm back in the water, nerves getting the best of me as I run back to the house.

* * *

The perfect smell of worn paper from books read over and over mixes with the aroma of fresh lattes being made when Henry and I walk into the Library Cafe. I know I was just here with Kyle, but it feels different with Henry. It feels *right.* It feels like *home.* I automatically wander over to the books, having not been able to really look at them when I was here with Kyle. Henry goes up to the counter to order for us. He doesn't even have to ask what I want. He just knows.

"Oh, welcome back! It's been so long since we've seen you! Is your friend with you?" The barista behind the counter instantly recognizes Henry, and I peek around the corner to wave as Henry points me out. *There's pure joy in his eyes. I can see it, and I can feel it.*

I meander over towards the back of the library section, reading the back of nearly every book that catches my eye. Between the distance I've made from the front counter and the sound of light chatter and espresso machines blending in with the baristas calling out names, I don't hear our own being called. I don't even know how long I've been looking at the books until Henry's arm reaches around me, an iced caramel latte now held in his hand between my chest and the bookshelf that I face in front of me. I gulp and take the coffee.

"I knew you'd get lost back here," Henry says as I turn around to face him. He takes a step back and leans up against the bookshelf behind him, one leg crossed over the other as he sips his iced Americano. I like to call it *coffee water.* My phone buzzes in my pocket, and I quickly take it out to check it, thinking it may be Clara. It's not.

Kyle: Hey! I just wanted to let you know I got back in early! Would love to take you out again before the end of the week!

I sigh and ignore Kyle's text, putting my phone back in my pocket. I'll just have to tell him I'm not interested the next time I see him.

"Who was that?" Henry asks, an eyebrow raised at me as I suddenly ignored a text.

"No one."

He squints his eye at me for a second before his gaze suddenly changes to that one look that I can't fully read yet. We stare on. The walls of books encapsulate both of us. Only about four feet apart... but all of a sudden it feels closer. A grin starts to form on his face before he nods his head towards the back of the library section and says, "Shall we?"

I smile with nostalgia, knowing exactly what he means, and I follow, feeling like a little kid yet again.

The back of the library looks exactly the same, and our special bean bag chair spot looks as if it hasn't been replaced since we were kids. Vintage. However, it does look smaller than I remember. The bean bag chair seemed huge when we were younger, and we always shared it without a second thought. Now, I feel suddenly nervous at the thought of sitting with him on it, but he plops down and immediately pats the spot next to him. I laugh nervously and slowly go to sit, our shoulders immediately touching. I don't move. Neither does he.

After a moment of silence, both sipping our drinks, Henry asks, "What's up with you? You're acting a little strange."

I mentally kick myself, knowing that I'm acting all nervous for no reason. *So what if I realized I might very well be in love with my best friend? Why does that have to change our traditions? Why does that have to make things weird? It doesn't... I hope.* I continue to second-guess myself. My confidence to tell him how I feel being drowned out by the fear of things changing between us, and not in a good way.

"Oh, it's just been a strange couple of days, that's all," I decide to say.

Henry nods. "Yeah, tell me about it."

"How did you end up leaving things with your dad?"

"Oh, you know." He shifts in his seat to face me more. I feel my heart skip a beat at the continued close proximity, my eyes fixed on his lips for only a second before he speaks again.

"He left and said I should think about all that I could do with his company. I said I was going to take the internship. He asked me to rethink it. He gave me a handshake, and he left. So, the usual."

My heart aches for him as he says this. I wish his Grandpa Joe were here to see him get accepted for the internship and decide to go. Joe would have cheered him on so much. He would have told everyone he knew about his grandson, the songwriter who made it in the Big Apple.

"I'm sorry," I say, looking him in the eyes and making sure that my gaze expresses that I truly mean it.

"Your Grandpa Joe would have been so proud. I am." He nods with a deep breath as he looks to the floor, and I know he knows that I mean every word. Silence fills the air again.

"August is almost over," I say, my thoughts spilling out of my head before I even realize.

"I know," Henry says, that unreadable look back behind his gaze. "What did you do the past couple of days when I was stuck with my dad?"

"Actually, I wrote a lot," I say, looking down again and beginning to play with my fingers. *This bean bag feels so small, I can barely look at him.*

"Really? That's awesome, El. I'm proud of you." His smile starts in his eyes this time, and I feel safe and seen. "Can I read some of what you wrote? Like old times?"

"Well, actually… I think I want to edit a few things before I finally show it to you, if that's okay?" His hand rests on my shoulder, and I hope he can't feel the goosebumps that immediately arise under his touch.

"Of course that's okay, El. Just whenever you're ready to share it, I'd be honored to read it." His hand leaves my shoulder, and I instantly crave more of his touch.

"Thanks," I say. "Have you written anything while we've been here?"

"Actually, yeah. When we had that writing session in my room, I finished the first assignment for my internship. It's a project everyone has to do before we get there. Write a song, and then on the first day, we all have to read one another's lyrics and guess who wrote the song. It's supposed to help us get to know each other and show how some songwriters have certain looks, while others might completely surprise you."

"Oh wow, that's really cool. You should send me a couple of the songs after you get there, and I'll try to guess which one is yours."

Henry laughs. "Okay, deal."

Silence again. The air thickening at the mention of his internship and assignments… and him *leaving*.

His new life starts in only a week. I want to tell him how I feel before he leaves… but the timing of it all threatens to make me bury my feelings for the sake of our friendship. Henry looks as if he's about to say something, when a familiar voice says my name.

"Elena?"

I jerk my head in the direction of the voice to see Kyle coming around the corner. I immediately feel guilty for ignoring his text just moments ago.

"Kyle! Hey, you're back!"

"Yeah! I actually texted you. You may not have seen it."

I see Henry's head jerk towards me in my peripheral vision. The realization that Kyle was the one whose text I had ignored earlier hits him.

"Oh, yeah, sorry," is all I can think to say.

"Is it cool if I join you two?" Kyle asks, and I look to Henry, pleading with my eyes for him to make up some excuse. But I know he won't. He couldn't even if he wanted to. That's not Henry.

"Yeah sure, man! Actually, you and Elena can catch up. I've got a couple of groceries to pick up for my mom to make dinner tonight, and I'm already cutting it close."

My heart sinks at the thought of him leaving. It sinks further at the thought of Kyle taking his place on this bean bag. Our special place for only *us*.

"I can pick you back up on my way back to the house?" Henry says, his eyes seeming as if they're searching for something within mine.

"Oh, don't worry about it, man. I can drop her off when we leave," Kyle says before I even get a chance to respond.

His gesture is so kind, but unwanted. Maybe now is going to be my time to just be upfront with him. I only have just over a week left, and I want to spend every moment I can with Henry.

Henry seems frozen in time for a moment before he stands and grabs his stuff, saying, "Oh great man, thanks."

He turns around and looks at me as he starts to leave, walking backwards for a moment behind Kyle.

"See ya, El," he says with a wink, and my stomach does a somersault. *What was that?* Henry fades away behind the rows of books, leaving Kyle standing in front of me. He starts to head for Henry's place next to me on the bean bag, and I immediately object.

"Actually!" I say, my voice coming out high and squeaky. I clear my throat before continuing and standing up. "Actually, would you mind if we moved to a table? I've been sitting here for a while, and my back kind of hurts."

"Oh, yeah sure!"

I sigh with relief and follow him to the table we shared the other day, towards the front of the cafe.

We take a seat, and the awkward silence rests between us immensely. *Okay, here goes nothing.*

"Kyle…"

"It's okay," he says, immediately interrupting me. I look at him, confused.

"I know," he says.

"Know what?"

"You and Henry?"

"Me and… wait…"

"It's okay, Elena. I've loved getting to hang out with you, and I wish we could get to know each other more… but I know love when I see it, and I won't ever stand in the way of that."

"How did you…" I begin to ask how he knew I loved Henry, mortified at the thought that I made it so obvious, but he answers my question before I even finish asking it.

"Anyone who sees the way he looks at you would know he's in love with you. I just hope he mans up to tell you soon if he hasn't."

I'm at a loss for words. I did not expect him to say that. *He thinks Henry's in love with me?*

I think back to Clara's many comments over the years about Henry pining for me. But, Kyle barely knows Henry, and he says he could see it by the way he looks at me? I replay the few gazes I haven't been able to read from Henry this August. The way his eyes fill with expressions that are altogether wild, raw, warm, and *new*. His pupils dilating as if dancing with a new emotion that I have yet to decipher behind his eyes. My mind is spinning, and I don't hear the next thing Kyle says. The muffled sound of his voice brings me out of my thoughts.

"Sorry… what did you say?"

He smiles. "I said, I have to get going soon. I'm taking my brother to dinner tonight. I just wanted to be sure and have one last moment alone with you before we parted ways."

I return his smile as he says this. "Thank you, Kyle. For everything. Really. I'm glad I was able to get to know you and have fun with you. I won't forget our date. Really. You're going to make some girl really happy one day."

His smile never leaves his face. "Thanks, Elena. I'm glad I met you, too."

There's a brief moment of silence before he saves us from any awkwardness threatening to fill the air. "Are you cool with leaving now?"

"Actually, I think I'll stay here for a little bit and write some. But you go ahead. I've done the walk from this cafe to the house a million times. I'll be fine."

He cocks his head to the side, and I realize I had never told him that I'd been coming to this cafe for years. I watch his expression change as he puts two and two together, but he doesn't say a thing about it.

He just smiles and lets out a little laugh as he checks again. "You sure you'll be okay?"

"Yeah. I'm good," I say with a smile. He sighs, and it's still genuine as ever. "Okay, well. See ya, Elena." He stands and pushes his chair in.

"See ya, Kyle."

He waves before turning around and leaving out the front door, and I watch him walk away. Thankful to have met him, and thankful that I didn't have to do much explaining.

As soon as he's out of sight, I pull out my notebooks from my bag. As I put the pen to paper, I pause again.

He could tell Henry was in love with me by how he looked at me. Thoughts and images turn into words, sentences, and similes in my mind, and before I know it, my pen can barely keep up with the words pouring from my heart.

* * *

I don't know how much time has gone by, but my thoughts stop flowing, and my hand stops scribbling down words at the loud and sudden clap of thunder. I look out the front window to see a torrential downpour begin.

"*Shoot,*" I whisper to myself.

I pull out my phone to check the radar and see that it says it's not expected to stop for at least the next two hours. It's currently 6:30 p.m. I should be getting back soon for dinner. I didn't realize I had been writing for nearly an hour. Putting my notebook and pen into my bag, I scoot in my chair and head towards the door. I keep watching the rain through the front window, waiting for it to magically stop. But it only begins to pour harder the longer I stare. I start to muster up the courage to make a run for it and see how far I can get before taking cover again, but when I look outside once more... I see Henry's car. His headlights flash twice, and my heart swells. I push the door open and run as fast as I can, puddles splashing with each step, before I open his passenger door, throw my bag to the floor, and slam the door shut as fast as I can.

I turn to look at him, and he smiles with a small laugh at my now drenched hair from the short run to his car.

"What are you doing here? Didn't you go get groceries?"

"Actually, I never left."

"What?" I look at him, dumbfounded.

"Well, when I got to the car, my mom texted me saying that she found what she needed at the house, and I didn't need to go to the store anymore. So, I was going to go back in, but I saw you and Kyle sitting at the table right inside. It seemed like you two were having a good conversation. I didn't want to interrupt, but I didn't want to leave... I don't know."

I stare at him in disbelief. Little did he know... the *good* conversation Kyle and I were having was one that indicated Henry was in love with me. He continues to explain more.

"I didn't wait that long before I eventually saw Kyle come out and leave without you. I was confused and was going to *finally* go back inside, but then I saw how focused you were on writing. You didn't look up from your notebook once until the rain started. I didn't want to interrupt your creative flow, but I wanted to make sure you got home safely. So, I waited. Scrolled on my phone. Just chilled really, it's no big deal."

I shake my head slowly at him, not even caring to hide the blush I feel rising to my cheeks anymore. My mouth breaks into a smile, and I lean forward to kiss Henry on the cheek. When I pull back, I see a blush now creeping to his face. The unreadable gaze now back in his eyes as they stay locked on mine... except now I know what the gaze resembles. It looks like *love*.

21

Chapter Twenty One

* * *

Another day came and went too fast, marking only seven full days left of August. Only seven more days left to breathe in the salty air. Seven more days left to catch the biggest waves. Seven more days left to make sure we visit the ice cream shop, walk on the pier, and bask in the warmth of the sun. *Seven more days until Henry leaves for New York. Seven more days to muster up the courage to tell him how I feel... or not.*

Today has been a perfect day so far. It started with the typical breakfast out on the balcony with Nana, Papa, and Clara. We all argued over the last couple of pieces of pineapple that still tastes so much better by the ocean. Nana said she'd run to the store to get one more for us to last us the rest of the week. I wish we could stay here forever. After breakfast, we met the whole Rolland clan on the beach for boogie boarding, reading, and tanning. We all rotated between the three all day, save for Clara, who hadn't bothered to open the book she brought once all August. She stayed either swimming in the water or lying on her towel, music blasting next to her. It was the perfect day. Simple and full of traditions. Just the way I like it. No one leaving, no interruptions, just our families and our ocean.

* * *

It's now just after dinner time, and Henry and I have made plans to meet in his room again for another writing session. I told him that I'd be bringing my own laptop and notebook this time, and not to expect to read anything I've written just yet. He said that was perfectly fine with him, and that he was just happy to be writing together again. I was, too. Walking up the stairs to his loft now, he opens the door at the sound of my footsteps. I pause in the middle of the stairs.

"Hey," I say, still feeling like a teenage girl again.

"Hey, come on up."

He opens the door and steps to the side, gesturing for me to come in. As I walk up the steps and enter his room, I can't help the smile that forms, threatening to make my cheeks sore later.

"Henry...what did you..."

"I figured we needed a really good writing session to make up for our lack... or should I say my lack of writing to you, and with you this past year."

I take in the scene before me. There are two comfortable, huge bean bags on the floor at the end of his bed. A little step stool is sitting between them with two steaming cups of tea and a bowl of popcorn mixed with M&M's. Sitting on each bean bag are lap desks that I've never seen before. He must have gone out to buy them. There's a candle burning on his bedside table, and it smells like warm vanilla and sugar. My favorite scent. There's a basket full of blankets placed in front of the bean bags, too. I look back over at Henry, his gaze also fixed on his setup. Eyes full of pride.

"You didn't have to do all of this," I say. His eyes shift to meet mine.

"Yeah, I did, though."

That look is back in his dark brown eyes, making them seem lighter all of a sudden. I'm transfixed on the golden specs in them as I remember what this gaze from him might mean. What Kyle swore it meant.

Henry speaks up, his eyes not blinking. Not moving from being locked into mine. "So, um, I never got to ask. How was your time with Kyle yesterday?"

I smile at his not-so-subtle interest in Kyle and me. "It was fine." I start to say.

Henry only nods, eyes unwavering from mine as they darken.

"We're just going to be friends."

There it is.

That look is back quicker than it seemed to disappear. His right eyebrow raises at the same time the corner of his mouth twitches slightly, fighting an obvious grin. "Oh yeah?"

"Yeah," I say.

And, we stand there in the door frame for a moment more, communicating with our eyes, the things we both seem too afraid to say.

* * *

An hour later, the bowl of popcorn and M&M's is nearly empty, and my tea is halfway gone. What remains now is cold. I've been writing nonstop since we finally left the doorway and started to focus on why we had come here in the first place. I've been writing and editing what I first drafted about a week ago, when Henry brought me here, demanding that I write whatever was on my mind. I hear him shift next to me ever so slightly, his head turning towards me in an attempt to peek over my shoulder at my laptop that rests on the lap-desk just above my knees. I immediately shift, turning the screen away from him, shooting him a glare.

"Hey… no peeking just yet."

He sighs and slumps back down into his bean bag chair in defeat, and I giggle at his eagerness.

"Well, can you at least give me a hint as to what you're writing about?"

I contemplate it for a moment, and then decide this is the perfect time to see how he *might* react to the word… before I actually have to tell him the truth about how I feel. *If I can ever muster up the courage.*

I turn towards him, his eyebrows rising as he notices that I'm about to answer his question. I make sure to meet his eyes with a serious and truthful gaze before I take a deep breath and utter the word.

"Love."

He doesn't look away, but simply grins the softest grin that begins in his eyes. He looks like he's about to say something when his phone rings, and I'm suddenly thankful for the interruption, because I'm not sure I'm ready for whatever he was going to say… or inquire. Everything I want to say is going straight from my brain to my keyboard. I've never really been good with spoken words. Written words have always been my preferred way of communicating anything. That's why I always loved when we would write our letters to each other. I wonder if he'll even have time to write to me from New York… or if he'll want to.

"Hold on, mom, slow down, slow down."

I'm broken free from my thoughts as Henry talks on the phone with his mom. I'm confused as to why she's calling him when she's only a house over, hanging out with Nana. I hear a muffled cry on the other end of the line and immediately close my laptop to turn my full attention to Henry. His eyebrows are knit together tightly, and he puts his forehead into his one free hand.

"It's going to be okay, Mom. Let me grab some of our things. Just take a deep breath, I'll meet you out at the car in ten."

I hear the line go dead, and Henry just places his phone to his side, staring at the wall in front of him, unmoving.

"Henry?"

With his eyes still focused on the wall, he responds in the most monotone voice that breaks a little as he says, "My dad's been in a car accident. He's just been transported to a hospital in New Jersey. That's all we know for right now. My mom and I are about to head to the airport to see if we can get the next flight out."

My breath hitches in my throat, and I silently pray that his dad is okay. Even though they have their issues, he's still family. Henry's dealt with so much loss already. He doesn't need more. He's still staring at the wall, but looks over at me with glossy eyes as I put my hand on his shoulder to break him from his trance. He blinks the tears away and takes a deep breath before he starts to say something else to me. His eyes are sad and tired as he gathers himself to utter words that aren't the ones I want to hear.

"I have to go. I'm sorry."

Tears well in my own eyes now, and one escapes to my cheek. He moves his hand as if he's going to wipe it, but I blot it with my sweatshirt sleeve before he has a chance, because if he makes even one delicate move with me right now, I'd break.

This is not in August's plans.

His hand falls back down between us as if it has fallen limp.

"It's okay," I say as I use all of my energy to muster up a smile. "Your mom needs you. You should be there for your dad. He needs you too... even if he doesn't say it. Everyone needs you in their lives, Henry."

A tear falls down his cheek now, and it takes everything in me not to reach up and wipe it away for him, too.

He sighs. "I'm going to get the first flight back as soon as I can, okay? I'm sure we'll get there, check on my dad, and everything will be okay, and I'll be able to get the first flight back tomorrow." It sounds as if he's trying to convince himself just as much as he's trying to convince me.

I simply nod. "Just… safe travels, okay? You can call me if you need to talk or… you can just call me if you want."

He nods at my offer, and before I can protest, he brings me in for a hug. I lose my breath as his arms tighten around my entire frame. My heart is breaking for him right now, and for the fact that he's having to leave our little slice of peace and comfort on this beach. It feels like it's against the rules of August. It feels like reality keeps trying to break its way into the one place where we've been able to escape from it every summer. Maybe… we're too old to escape from reality now. No matter how many cliffs we jump off of or movies we watch. No matter how many times we boogie board or visit our special spot in the Library Cafe from when we were kids… the truth is… we aren't kids. We never would be again.

His hand rubs circles into my back as I choke out a single sob, and this is when I decide to pull back and collect myself. This isn't about me.

"Go," I say, wiping the tear from his cheek now, not caring about the delicate touches anymore.

He doesn't say anything, but his eyes fill with the expression that looks like the one word I uttered just moments ago. The word that's been hanging in the thick air between us for maybe as long as we've ever known each other.

"You can stay here. Write as long as you need to."

I only nod as he says this, and then I watch him get up and silently throw things into a duffel bag before he finally walks to the door frame that we stood in together only an hour ago, having no idea how this night would turn out. I'm sure we thought that by now, we'd be making ourselves decaf coffee or taking a ten-minute writing break to play a game of cards. He turns back around to look at me one last time, forces a smile and a sad wave, and then heads down the stairs. I wait until I hear the front door shut before I let the rest of the tears I'd been fighting begin to fall freely.

22

Chapter Twenty Two

* * *

It's been two days since Henry left me in his room that night. After I collected myself, I finally started to write again. It was the only way left that I could escape reality, August seeming to fail me once more. I woke up before dawn the morning after Henry had left, to the sound of Clara barging into his room. She said nothing, but just crawled into bed with me, both of us falling back asleep quickly. I assumed Jason had told her what was going on, but when we both finally woke up a few hours later into the morning, she told me Jason had gone with Henry and Jules to help out with anything they may need. We spent the rest of that day watching movies with Nana and Papa, walking on the pier together, and getting ice cream. Nana and Papa were both saddened by the news when they heard it, Nana for Jules especially. I know they also love the traditions and peace that come with our trips each August. They've always understood my want to just escape, be a kid, and forget the rest of the world.

Henry hasn't called once since he arrived in New Jersey. He texted me once he got there to say that things were hectic and he'd get back as soon as he could, but that was it, and that was two days ago. Jules called Nana this morning, saying that Mr. Rolland was going to be fine, but he got lucky and would definitely be needing physical therapy for a while. I wondered why Henry didn't tell me that himself.

Right now, Clara and I are at the Library Cafe. She agreed to come with me, even though she's more of a grab-and-go type of person when it comes to coffee. It had been raining all morning, so it worked as an incentive for her to come and get out of the house. I've been jotting down ideas for how to finish what I had been writing, but my brain is all jumbled.

I scribble through a word as I misspell it for the fifth time. Instead of words flowing through my brain and onto the paper, all I hear is a ticking time bomb. With each tick that goes by, I can feel the end of August getting closer and closer. I sigh as the sunlight pours in through the window, reflecting onto my notebook and creating a hue that allows me to see all the tiny dust particles floating through the air. It's amazing what new things you can see when you shine a little light on it. Things you may have never noticed before, but that were always there. That's how I feel about my love for Henry. It's as if it were always there, but went unseen until just the right amount of light had shone on it.

I think back to the conversation I had here with Kyle that already feels like a lifetime ago. He shed light on the fact that Henry may feel the same way, not even really knowing Henry himself. I imagine the look that I had been seeing from Henry all summer again, his eyes so intense each time. I couldn't really read into what he might have been saying with his gaze until Kyle shed light on it… and now I'm just hoping one of us is able to have the chance… the *time* to say it with our words instead.

"Ellie… can we please go now? The sun is *finally* out!" Clara asks me, holding out the word 'finally' as if to beg. I close my notebook instantly, my brain too jumbled to even begin to put sentences together.

"Yeah. I'm done for the day. Let's go."

Clara jumps up, the promise of soaking up some vitamin D instantly boosting her mood. As I open the front door to the cafe and step out into the light, it does the same for me. The sky is perfectly blue, and the summer air is perfectly warm with a slight breeze diminishing the humidity. I close my eyes and angle my face towards the sky, allowing myself to bask in the warmth of the sun for a moment.

One more day. He'll be back in one more day, and then we can enjoy all the time we have left.

* * *

As Clara and I walk out to the beach just under an hour later, I see that Nana and Papa are already sitting with their umbrellas out and a full beach bag between both of their chairs. When we approach, Papa turns his head instantly. "There you two are! Perfect timing, the sky's completely clear now, and the waves look good for boogie boarding."

"Okay, wanna see who can catch the biggest wave again?" Clara asks Papa as she grabs her board, which he's already brought out for her.

"Only if you promise not to be a sore loser," Papa says, grabbing his own board.

His and Clara's laughter fades as they walk towards the ocean, and I take a seat in Papa's now-empty chair next to Nana, grabbing what's left to read of my Emily Henry book. I sigh, and it must have been bigger than I thought because Nana abruptly closes her book, turning her position to me. I mark my place in mine before turning to face her.

"You should tell him, Ellie." I'm surprised by her sudden directness, and I don't know what to say before she continues.

"It's your life, but listen, dear. If he feels the same way and neither one of you ever says anything… you're only robbing yourselves of something that could be the greatest blessing of your lives. Don't rob each other of the free gift that is love. It's a wonderful thing to be known and loved by your best friend… and it's even more wonderful when that love turns into a partner by your side through both the wonderful and harder times in life."

She looks out at the water as Papa is swimming over to grab his boogie board that has just escaped him, her eyes full of love. It looks similar to the look Henry has been giving me… only confirming what I think I know but am afraid to say. To confront. She turns back to look at me as I wipe a tear from my cheek. She then reaches over to pat my hand while giving me a big smile.

"It'll all work out," she says.

And I hold on to the fact that she seems to genuinely believe that it would, because I wasn't so sure.

* * *

I jolt awake at the sudden sound of my phone buzzing in the middle of the night, my anxiety immediately skyrocketing. Shuffling over to the other side of my bed, I grab my phone from the nightstand. Clara groans at the sound of it buzzing awfully loudly. It's Henry. Calling at nearly 2:00 a.m. I take a deep breath before answering in a hushed tone.

"Henry? Hey, is everything okay?"

"Yeah, sorry to wake you." His voice sounds heavy as his words rush out.

"No, it's fine," I say again, whispering. Clara groans again, and I roll my eyes. No matter what time it is, you do not want to be the one to disrupt her sleep.

"Hold on one second," I whisper into the phone.

"Sure, okay," Henry says as I quietly make my way downstairs and out onto the back patio.

I gasp at the full moon that is centered perfectly above the vast ocean that now blends in with the night sky. The only proof of the ocean being there is now the sound of the waves breaking and the moonlight and stars illuminating the whitecaps that form.

"Okay," I say in a normal volume now. "I can talk now."

"Okay," is all Henry says. I'm not sure what to say next, and he's the one who called me in the middle of the night, so I wait. He sighs, and I can hear the heaviness behind his breath again before he finally talks more.

"So, my dad's recovery is going to take a lot longer than we'd hoped. He's going to stay in the hospital to be monitored for a few more days, just to make sure there's no further internal bleeding." I cringe at the thought. He was really lucky.

Henry continues. "My mom is going to stay with him the next couple of days, and then they're going to start physical therapy up here in Jersey and stay with one of my dad's co-workers until he's healed enough to travel back home to South Carolina."

My heart aches. "Oh, wow. I'm sorry I won't be able to say bye to Jules, but I understand." My heart breaks even more as the words make it more real. August is ending. Time has run out.

"I'll have to send a gift or get a new book for Jules or something for you to take back to her when you see her." There's silence on the other end of the line after I say this. I can only hear his slowed breaths before another long sigh comes.

"Elena," he says, and I gulp. He never calls me by my full name. Ever.

"I'm not coming back."

My aching heart immediately shatters as the ticking time bomb in my mind finally explodes.

23

Chapter Twenty Three

* * *

"El?" I hear his voice, but I can't say anything. I don't know how to speak. He would definitely be able to hear how heartbroken I am by the sound of my voice, and I don't want to add to the burdens he's already carrying.

"El?" He says again.

"Mhm?"

Another sigh is heard on the other end of the line as I fail to hide how upset I am.

"I'm sorry," he says. "It's just that… my mom's going to need me here the next couple of days, or she won't get any sleep. She's tending to my dad day and night, even though the doctors and nurses say she needs her rest too. She says that she wants family at his side at all times… so that leaves me to be the only one to relieve her and force her to get some rest at the hotel."

It's my turn to sigh now, and I do as I realize there's no way Henry would ever leave his mom's side. And he shouldn't. Even though Henry left me hanging when Grandpa Joe passed, I heard from Nana that he was hovering over Jules left and right, always making sure that she was resting enough, eating enough, and laughing enough in the midst of her grief. I wonder who did that for him amid his grief. *I would have if he had let me. And, I'd leave my favorite place on earth right now if he told me he wanted me there with him.* But he doesn't ask me to come.

Instead, he tells me that it makes the most sense for him to stay there with his mom, help out, and then take the ferry over to New York at the end of the week to move into his apartment before his internship starts. I know this all makes sense in my head as he explains everything, but my heart rejects each word he says. Silence is resting on either end of the phone, the only sound is my shaky breath as I fight back the tears once again.

"I promise to write to you this time, and I promise I'll come visit you as soon as I can."

"Okay, yeah," I say, trying to convince myself that he will.

But I think back to this past year and all of the unrequited letters I'd sent. I think about how he'll be getting a small internship salary, and how there's no way he'll be able to pay for New York rent, food, subway fees, and a flight to see me in Colorado. I feel August and all of its promises slipping through my fingers.

"I'm really sorry, El."

"Don't apologize," I say, my voice cracking a little as I try to hide the fact that tears have already escaped. "You're where you need to be. It's okay, just… should I let everyone know?"

"No. It's okay. My mom is going to call Nana in the morning. I just… I wanted you to hear it from me first."

"Okay… thanks."

Silence sits between us for another moment.

"Yeah."

As he says this, I can almost hear a slight break in his voice, and I wonder if he's fighting back tears the same way that I am.

I look up at the moon again, once more, wondering if he's back at the hotel, in a hospital wing, or outside looking at the moon too. The only thing that we could both experience together from this distance.

"I guess I'll say bye to the ocean for you then," I say as I focus on the glistening water beneath the stars now. We used to always say goodbye to the ocean together on the last morning of each trip. He would wake me up at sunrise, and we'd spend every last moment we could by the water.

He lets out a breath, and I can't tell if it's a laugh or the sound of his heart breaking, too.

"Yeah. Make sure to tell the ocean that I'll miss it. So, so much."

Something in me tells me that he's not talking about the ocean, and I know that I'm not either, as I say, "I'll miss it, so much too."

24

Chapter Twenty Four

* * *

I don't remember falling back asleep after my phone call with Henry early this morning. I'm awoken by the sound of the sliding glass door, and I immediately regret not going back up to bed. I couldn't. I didn't want Clara to hear me crying. I guess I must have dozed off, choosing the most uncomfortable position in one of our lounge chairs on the porch. As I see Clara coming out onto the deck, I rub my stiff neck, slowly sitting up.

"Jason just called," Clara says in a small voice. That's all she has to say to confirm she knows, and she doesn't question why I was out here all night as she walks over to take a seat next to me. She looks at me as if she's waiting for me to say something, or cry… except I have no energy left in me. I simply shrug my shoulders, and she pulls me into a hug. She's not usually one to hug, so I savor every moment… because I need it.

We break apart at the sound of Nana and Papa coming to join us. Nana walks over to me with a soft smile. She just simply kisses the top of my head before handing me a mug of freshly brewed coffee. I inhale the strong scent and instantly feel more awake with the smell alone.

Taking a sip, I sigh and look out at the ocean. Usually, the ocean could always make my problems seem smaller. Now I see it as the problem. This ocean. This beach. This house. This town. This month. It's not the same without Henry and Jules. It's not even the same without Jason… and it hasn't been the same since the last time we were all here together…with Grandpa Joe. He was the one who got the house next door for Henry and Jules once Henry's dad started traveling so much for work. He was the one who started fishing with Papa and introduced Henry and me. I'm starting to think that he may have been the glue holding every summer together, and that his absence has shifted something in how August feels.

I take another sip of coffee, savoring the warmth it brings me. We're all just sipping our drinks, steam above every mug as we take in the beautiful ocean before us. It seems as if no one knows what to say. That is, until Papa breaks the silence.

"You know what? Today seems like a great morning for a family bike ride."

We all exchange smiles, perking up at the idea.

"Sounds perfect, Papa," I say.

We all finish our coffees, change out of our pajamas, and meet outside to do one of the very first things we ever did here together, when it was just the four of us, and I'm thankful to still have this tradition. As we all start to pedal and head on our way towards the path that follows between the ocean and the bay, I soak in the feeling… because this moment right here… this is how August is supposed to feel.

* * *

We've been biking for about twenty minutes, with no specific destination in sight, and I've been taking in every ounce of scenery around me. The vast bodies of water on either side of us, the thin grass that is sacred to the sandy beaches, and seagulls flying overhead. I relish in this setting, my hair blowing in the wind, an arm outstretched to the side as I guide my bike with the other. I'm feeling better than I was this morning. The coffee has its full effect on me now, and the Vitamin D mixed with salty air acts as a bandage for my wounded heart. Even the worst days are better at the beach, and I'm thankful I'm experiencing a sad day surrounded by the ocean with my family by my side. My mind wanders to Henry. I wonder if he feels alone. Clara mentioned earlier that Jason would be on his way back soon to drive the Rolland's car back to South Carolina, and I know Jules is probably waiting on Mr. Rolland's hand and foot. Who is taking care of Henry?

The thought saddens me a bit more before we begin down a path that follows condos for miles and miles, lining the beach. We pass one that we had stayed in for a couple of years before getting the beach house. Back when it was just the four of us. I had no idea what these trips... what the month of August would eventually mean to me. *What Henry would eventually mean to me.* I just hope one day, I have a chance to truly tell him. I shift my focus at the sound of Clara's voice, who's a few feet ahead of me, my thoughts having slowed down my pace as I let memories play on a reel in my mind.

"Let's bike towards ice cream!" She shouts back at me.

I give her a thumbs up, pedaling a bit faster at the thought of chocolate ice cream and a fresh waffle cone. There is no better comfort treat.

* * *

After getting back to the house, Papa excuses himself for an afternoon nap, while Nana dives back into her book on the back porch. Clara and I head upstairs, and as we do, her phone rings.

"Jason, hey!" She says with enthusiasm, a smile bigger than she even realizes showing up on her face.

I start to gather up my notebook and laptop into my bag as she continues to talk to him. She laughs at something he says, and I turn to hide my smile. She sounds like a little kid. She hangs up and is silent for a moment before letting me in on what was said.

"He'll be here soon. He just boarded his flight. I think I'm going to take the car to pick him up." She sounds timid, as if she's tiptoeing around the words she says, obviously feeling guilty because she's about to see Jason again… and there's no telling when I'll see Henry again. I finish assembling things into my bag and turn to face her.

"Clara, it's okay. I'll be fine, okay? Maybe this is what was supposed to happen." Clara begins to shake her head in protest, but I speak up again before she has the chance to.

"I'm just going to use the time left here to pour myself into my writing, okay? Take the car keys," I say as I toss them over to her. "I'm going to walk to the Library Cafe, and I'll probably be there for a while. So, don't wait up. Just let me know when it's time for dinner."

I force a smile that I know she can see straight through. She looks at me with pity as I head to the door.

"You sure you don't want to come with me to the airport?"

"Yeah. I'm sure. I just want to be alone with myself and my thoughts for a while. See what I can put into written words on paper."

Clara nods with a sad yet understanding smile, and I make my way downstairs and out the door before I let one tear escape. After the one finally makes its way down my cheek, I wipe my eyes, take a deep breath, and walk forward… hoping to move forward as I do.

* * *

As I settle into the coffee shop, sipping on my favorite iced caramel latte, I stare at my piece on love. Reading it over and over, I wish it were something that I was able to show Henry in person. I could picture his eyes looking into mine with every realization as he would read it. I could picture my palms sweaty, my heart pounding as I anticipated his reaction. Now, I just have it for myself. It's proof that I had it in me. The words, the story, the longing. The more I re-read it, the more I suddenly feel a sense of pride. *I wrote this, straight from the heart.* If no one else ever reads it, at least I'll know that I wrote it, and it means something.

I open up another tab with an empty document. The cursor blinks as I rack my brain for what I should write about next. It suddenly dawns on me that I do want someone else to see my writing. Not just me. Not just Henry. I want anyone who cares to read what I write to see my work. To imagine the imagery that I place on the pages. To feel seen and escape from reality, a new world forming in their minds as they take in each word. I was able to finally write for myself again this summer… but why should I limit myself to just that?

I think of Henry and his internship. He could easily just write songs and never do anything with them, keeping his art to himself. But he sought to show it to the world. To learn more and nurture his talent, seeking to be successful with something he's passionate about. I've always admired his diligence and aspirations in that way. I've just always been too afraid to do that myself. I always felt as if my writing wasn't good enough or was too vulnerable for me to share. But what if my writing was exactly what someone else needed? Was it selfish for me to keep it all to myself? Was it cowardly of me not to even *try* to pursue something that I'm passionate about?

Before I can think even more, I'm opening up a new tab to Google. I immediately start to search for writing internships. The first one that pops up makes my breath hitch in the back of my throat.

The New Yorker Magazine: Creative and Fiction Writing Intern Wanted Immediately!

I hold my breath as I click on the link. It brings me to a special page on the careers section of *The New Yorker's* website.

"Last-minute intern needed, as we have an unexpected extra spot. Accepting applications immediately. Please apply with your resume and writing samples below, and we will reach out to you as soon as possible if your specifications meet our requirements/needs for this position."

My cursor hovers over the huge "APPLY" button.

The New Yorker. I could never be good enough for the New Yorker, right? I only just found my voice again.

I shake my head at the thought, realizing that this is such a great opportunity, and the least I can do is try. Take a step of faith. Out of my comfort zone. Discomfort produces movement.

There's a 99% chance this will probably lead nowhere, and they'll choose someone who is *way* more qualified. They may have even already chosen someone. They may be looking at the candidate that they want to bring onto the team right now, and applying could very well be a waste of my time. But... there also might be a small chance that they'd see my resume and writing samples... *and feel like taking a chance on me*. They may feel my passion in the words that I write. I read more and audibly gasp as I learn that the chosen participant would be flown out to New York at the very end of August if accepted, and the person would need to be flexible as they need to fill this position suddenly and immediately.

I must have been reading this part aloud to myself, because I earn a judgemental glance from the woman at the table next to me as I finish. I don't care, though. I re-read it once more to make sure I'm understanding it correctly. *This is wild.* There's a chance... a slim one... but still. There's a chance I could spend the next year alongside Henry in New York City as we both pursue our passions. There's a chance I could write for other people, and not just for myself. There's a chance I could make something of this passion I have. And, there's a chance I could tell Henry how I truly feel... and as soon as *next week.*

I shake my head, my stomach full of butterflies. Even a small chance... is still a chance. I think back to Nana's words from the other day. *If you don't try... you'll never know.* She was referring to Henry, but I think it certainly applies to this situation. To any leap of faith in life, really. I take a deep breath, the cursor still hovering over the button. I mentally count to three in my head before clicking "APPLY."

* * *

On my way back from the Library Cafe, I feel giddy. I know the chance is slim, but I'm proud of myself for taking the chance. I used my most recent piece on love as part of my writing samples. I polished it up, and was equally satisfied, nervous, and ecstatic when I finally hit submit. I'm so lost in my thoughts as I begin to walk up the driveway to my house, until I hear quiet giggles coming from the Rollands' front porch. I walk over to see what's going on, and my jaw nearly reaches the ground as I turn the corner to see Jason and Clara on the front porch, Clara's hands wrapped around Jason's neck, his at her waist, and both of their lips locked... in a kiss.

25

Chapter Twenty Five

* * *

I audibly gasp, taking a quick step back, only to run backwards into the mailbox. A loud thud sounds, and I hear Clara yelp. Grabbing my elbow and wincing with the contact, I turn back around the corner, *busted*. Clara is now nearly on the other side of the porch, her hands clasped together at her chest. Jason stands where he originally was, leaning against the post, one leg crossed over the other with a smug grin as he tries to hide his amusement. I am doing the same as I say nothing, but watch Clara mutter a quick goodnight to Jason before marching down the front steps and immediately jogging past me and into our house. I follow behind her, getting my laughter out while I can.

When I open the door, Clara is standing in the sitting room to the left, hands on her hips, glaring at Nana.

"I didn't see anything more than a peck! What scared you off so quickly?"

I begin laughing at Nana's choice of words. She obviously just got caught spying on Clara through the corner window near the fireplace that shows a direct line to the side of the Rollands' front porch.

Clara points to me with an aggressive thrust of her arm. "*She* scared me off!"

I place my hand to my chest in a mocking way. Jaw dropping as if to act innocent. "Me? I didn't say a word!"

Clara stomps over to the chair in the corner by the window, sinking into her seat.

"You didn't have to," she says in a small voice.

Nana walks over to the edge of the chair and starts to play with Clara's hair. *The best feeling.*

"Oh dear, well, from what I could see… it looked like a good kiss. Was it a good kiss?" Nana asks, looking around from where she stands behind to see Clara's face just as she brings her hands up to cover her obvious blush.

"Nana!" She sinks lower into the chair.

I walk over in a fit of giggles, taking a seat on the arm of the chair. "So?"

Clara removes her hands from her face with a sigh, cheeks still red, mouth fighting a smile.

"Come on, tell us!" Nana adds.

It feels like we're just a few teenage girls gossiping about boys, and I take in the scene, thankful to have this special bond with my little sister and my grandmother. Clara moves to sit up right in the chair again. She slaps her hands on her thighs as she begins to tell us how this happened.

"Well, he took me to brunch today. He remembered how I had mentioned there was a new breakfast place that I had been wanting to try. He paid for my meal, and then we went for a walk on the beach. He told me that he likes me a lot and that he wanted to get to know me more… to see if we could *be more*." Nana starts to rub Clara's back.

"Well, it seems you two decided to *be more*, huh?" Nana teases her again, and Clara glares with a grin.

"Well, I said I wanted to get to know him more, too… and that we'd see where it goes. But then we just ended up playing a bunch of board games at the Rollands' house, and I realized that I really liked him too. I just didn't want to admit it. I'm not one for all the lovey-dovey words and stuff."

"Oh, we know," I say as a joke, running my fingers through her hair.

"So," she continues. "I was just trying to tell him when we were leaving that I felt the same, and he was really great and blah, blah, blah. I couldn't figure out how to say it, so he basically shut me up as I stumbled over my words. He literally interrupted me in the middle of my struggle to convey my feelings and asked if it was okay if he kissed me… and I said yes, so he did."

"And?" Nana pushes farther, earning yet another glare, followed by a giggle before Clara hides her face again.

"And it was amazing, okay? There!" Clara sinks back into the chair yet again.

Nana laughs with the widest grin as she pats Clara's back, and I feel equally joyful and sorrowful as I see my sister finally begin to open up her heart. I know it's not easy for her. That's why I didn't really push her too much on the whole discussion of Jason this summer. I knew it would work out if it was meant to, and it seems it just might. I feel tears start to brim in my eyes, and I quickly blink them away, not wanting to make this moment about me. I just wish Henry were here so I could open up my heart to him. I'm sure he'll hear about this whole ordeal from Jason, and I need to make sure Henry knows that I'm team Clara, and Jason better treat her right.

"Not to bring down the mood," I say, "but when does Jason leave?"

Clara sighs, sitting back up once again. "He leaves the day we do, just much earlier. He's going to drive back to South Carolina, and he said that once I move down to North Carolina for NC State in the fall, he wants to take me out on a real date."

I smile widely, genuinely happy for my sister. "That's great, Clara. That's *really* great." Clara's expression falters a bit as she must notice the shakiness in my voice. We hadn't really talked about Clara moving for college at all this summer. I've been trying to ignore all the changes that were bound to come after this August passed. I'm scared. Henry's already gone, and soon Clara will be too. Both so far away... my two best friends.

Clara doesn't say anything, but instead moves to hug me. I've gotten more hugs from her this August than any other. Nana reaches around us both, playing with our hair, and I savor the feeling. This moment. This August. This house. My family.

Footsteps sound from the living room, and Papa comes around the corner.

"What's with all this hugging?"

Clara, Nana, and I share a brief glance, seeming to have the same idea before we all run over to Papa, forcing him into a group hug, and it's the safest and warmest feeling I've felt in the past couple of days.

26

Chapter Twenty Six

* * *

The next few days come and go in a blur. Moments of boogie boarding, short calls with Henry when he was free, soaking in the sun, and walking on the pier with melting ice cream cones filled the last few memories we would make this August. We all woke up before dawn this morning to finish packing the last few things and enjoy as much of the morning as we could before we left. We always rented a car from the Birmingham, Alabama, airport and drove the rest of the way every year. We'd be catching our flights back to Colorado early tomorrow morning, so we still have a few hours left to soak up every moment we can here before heading to our hotel in Birmingham.

I watched from our upstairs bedroom window this morning as Clara said goodbye to Jason in the driveway. They only hugged this time, a long hug that had Clara stretched on her tip toes. She came back inside, giddy and seemingly satisfied with how they left things. She said they'd agreed to talk every day, but also to take things slow. He had told her to be ready for their date in a few weeks. My heart ached as she said that.

A few weeks. That's all that's left until my little sister moves nearly twenty-six hours away, and loneliness will threaten to loom over me again.

* * *

The rest of the early hours this morning were spent checking under beds, in closets, and in drawers for any items we may have missed. I'm checking the bathroom one more time when Clara comes barging in.

"Okay. You've checked enough. We'll do another sweep before we leave. Come say goodbye to the ocean with me."

I sigh, thinking back to how Henry had told me to do this for him when we spoke on the phone only a few nights ago. I nod, quickly opening my unzipped suitcase to grab my book and beach towel that rests on top, and then we both run down the stairs like little kids to greet the ocean, as if it were the first day we got down here, only this time when we leave to come in from the beach… we won't be coming back.

* * *

After a few minutes of wading in the water and looking for seashells, stuffing them into our pockets to add to our overflowing collections at home, Clara decides to go for a walk along the water. I opt to join Nana in her extra beach chair, Papa having gone back inside to make sure everything's packed away thoroughly. I grab my book and get comfortable. Looking over to see that Nana is nearly to the end of her book, I flip to the next chapter of mine and notice I've almost finished mine too. We say nothing, both escaping into our books, racing to finish them before we leave the most perfect place to read. I breathe in the salty air and enjoy the peaceful sounds of the waves as I am immediately transported back to Emily Henry's North Bear Shores, anticipating the perfect ending.

I pause as I read, taking a second to look out to the vast ocean. I wonder how many people have sat on a beach reading this book… and I wonder if someday, somebody somewhere would find what I write to be worth reading next to a beautiful scene like the one before my eyes. My mind wanders back to the internship I applied for. I hadn't heard anything. I shouldn't get my hopes up. But, as I focus back on the book, the wind threatening to turn the pages before I'm ready, I start to think of all the things I might like to put in a book of my own one day. The idea feels like a distant dream that I want to chase down, bringing it closer to reality… ready to turn the page on my life.

Nana and I both finish our books within mere seconds of each other. We both sigh, looking at the ocean. "How was your book?" I ask her.

"Oh, just the perfect beach read. How was yours?"

I laugh and show her the cover. "Oh, well, yours must have really been the *perfect beach read,* then."

I laugh at her joke, nodding. "Yeah. I think I might like to write a book one day."

"Well, if you do, make me a character in it!" Papa's voice chimes from behind me, having snuck up on our conversation.

"I'll get right on that." I laugh.

Papa grins, then looks out to the ocean. He whistles, signaling for Clara to get up. She must've gotten back from her walk a while ago. Her head comes up from where it's rested in her crossed arms, stomach to the sand, getting one last good tanning session in. She slowly gets up and makes her way over.

"You two ready to go say bye to the ocean?"

My shoulders shrug, a weight feeling as if it's just fallen onto either one.

With a sigh, I say, "Yeah. Let's go."

And, just like that, Papa, Clara, and I are all three standing side by side, our feet sinking deeper into the sand with each wave that washes over them, yet again. I take a picture with my phone and send a quick text to Henry. We still have never been much of the texting type, but I told him I'd say goodbye for him. I take in the sight before me, sunrays beaming on the calm blue waves.

"Until next time," Papa says.

"Yeah… until next time," I say, wondering if next August will keep its promises better than this one.

* * *

Henry hasn't responded to my text, but I send him another one as we make one last stop at the Library Cafe before officially hitting the road. I take a picture of my iced latte, holding it up in front of our bean bag spot in the far corner. I try to think of something to say, but end up just sending the picture with no caption. Putting my phone back into my pocket, I admire our special spot one last time, thinking of how many times we've come here together over the years. We always got lucky, as no one else would ever be sitting in these chairs. Probably because they were so far in a corner, they're easy to miss.

My phone starts to ring, and I dig it out of my pocket so fast I almost drop it. Henry's name lights up on my screen as the FaceTime call comes in. My stomach fills with butterflies as I hit answer. The butterflies only multiply at the sight of his face. It looks like he's outside of a house. I don't recognize it.

"Hey, stranger," he says with a grin. I can see the tiredness in his eyes through the screen, but they're still just as warm as ever.

"Hey, I was about to file a missing persons report on you."

He gives a shy laugh. "Sorry, I know I've been M.I.A. It's just been a little crazy over here. I'm at my dad's coworker's house right now. Mom sent me on a bunch of errands to get his guest room all set up with things he may need if he gets bored. Things like his laptop, all his chargers, and even things to stock the mini fridge."

"The guest room has a mini fridge?" I ask.

"Oh… every guest room has a mini fridge."

"*Every*? How many are there?"

"There's a whole floor dedicated to just *guests*." He says, and I gape, jaw dropping.

"Wow… what do your dad and his co-workers do again?"

Henry laughs again. "Nothing you'd be interested in, and nothing I like to talk about… but they do make good money. I'll give them that."

There's silence for a moment, and I see a flicker of sadness in his eyes.

"How have things been with your dad?"

He shrugs. "Fine, I guess. I think Mom talked to him because he hasn't mentioned anything negative about the internship since we've been here. We just don't discuss it. Or his work, really. It's better that way."

I nod, and then he changes the subject, and I don't mind it.

"I move into my apartment in like two days."

My heart sinks, and I'm glad we're only on FaceTime, so he can't see how my shoulders instantly drop.

"Wow," I say. "That's super cool. You'll have to send me pictures."

"I will. I promise," he says.

I want to stay on the phone with him forever, but Nana calls from the front of the aisle of books I'm currently standing in. "You ready, sweetie?"

"Is that Nana?" Henry asks.

"Yeah," I say. "We're about to hit the road." I notice that Henry's shoulders fall too, his phone showing more of his body as his longer arm is outstretched.

"Okay, well, keep me updated. Tell everyone I say hello and safe travels."

There's so much more I wish I could say to him, but all I say is, "Thanks. I will. See ya, Henry."

At that, he sighs, seeming as if there's so much more he wants to say, too, but all he says is, "See ya, El."

And with that, I hang up, shoving my phone into my pocket and walking towards the exit, not daring to look back at our special spot, because I have to leave it behind with my unsaid feelings and unmet promises.

* * *

I watch as we pass by the pier, thinking back to that night in early August when I had to drive Henry to the urgent care. I watch as we pass the ice cream shop, immediately wanting one last chocolate ice cream cone. We pass the arcade and the movie theater, and I think of my brief time with Kyle and hope that he's well. Then, we end up passing the sushi restaurant I took Henry to, and I huff a silent laugh as I think of him hiding the fact that he indeed liked sushi. Finally, just before getting on the interstate, we pass the rocks we hiked and jumped off of together. The moment replays in my mind as I watch two people jump hand-in-hand right before we pass it fully, leaving it behind. But the memory stays on a loop in my mind as we merge onto the busy highway. The feeling of Henry's hands around my waist is forever ingrained in my mind as if it just happened. I sigh, wishing so badly that I could just be near him again, talk to him face to face, tell him about every fear and every dream and every aspiration I have for writing now, for life… for *love*.

I grab my phone and scroll through my emails to check if there has been anything I missed from *The New Yorker.* Nothing. Feeling defeated, I go back to the Google search bar, typing in the internship name to see if anyone else had gotten accepted. There's a brief subheader under the article when it finally loads.

No longer accepting applications.

The defeat fully sinks in as I read this. I lock my phone and throw it down in the middle seat between Clara and me. I feel her look over to me at the sudden impact of it, but I just turn up my music and stare out the window… not in the mood to discuss my failure. My failure to try and seize opportunities like this before it's too late. My failure to tell Henry how I feel before it was too late. I watch as palm trees pass, thinking about how sad I'd always been to leave the beach every summer because of all the fun we'd had together. Now, however, I'm sad to leave all of the missed opportunities, things left unsaid, and promises unmet. There's only a couple of days left in August, and my hope that things will start to turn around wears thinner and thinner as we get farther and farther from my favorite escape, and closer and closer to reality and the changes that await.

* * *

The hours filled with hotel stays and airport check-ins leave just as fast as they came, and suddenly we're pulling into the driveway of my childhood home. Papa is pulling our luggage from the back before I can even get out of the car. They had opted to park it at a friend's house near the airport, making it easier to drive us home themselves. Papa is anxious to return to his routine as he places the bags orderly in front of us. Clara and I take turns hugging Nana and Papa both.

"We'll see you both for Saturday breakfast in just a few days, okay? Got to soak up the few Saturdays we have left with this one," Nana says, squeezing Clara as I hug onto Papa tightly. We say our 'love yous,' and head inside.

Papa waves out the window as he drives away, and Mama comes out to greet us.

"Did you two have fun?" I immediately run into my mother's arms as she asks this.

"Oh goodness," she says at the impact of my hug. Her hugs have always been my favorite. It's like the world falls silent when I'm hugging my mom, and I know that no matter what, I'm safe right there in her arms.

"We have a lot to update you on," Clara says from the other side, as Mama brings her in to hug her too. I instantly feel the instinct to push my feelings down, not wanting to talk about all the great things that made the end of this summer so much harder. Not wanting to talk about the hard things that made it different, too. A tear escapes my cheek, though, and our mom turns my cheek to make eye contact with me.

"Elena?"

"Henry's in New York," is all I say.

She doesn't push further or ask what this means. All she does is bring me back into the safety of her hug, rubbing my back as she tells me it's all going to be okay. My shoulders start to feel lighter, the warmth of my mother's hug reminding me that I'm not alone. I'll tell her more about everything later, but I decide in this moment to lighten the mood as I collect myself.

"Clara met a boy," I whisper just loud enough for Clara to hear from beside me as I continue to hug our mom. Mama pushes me from her, arms extended to both of my shoulders as she gapes at me and then turns to face Clara.

"Oh, did she now?" Clara glares at me, and I laugh as she lightly hits me on the shoulder.

"Well, come inside and eat, and tell me *everything,*" Mama says as she ushers us in.

The smell of clean laundry and fresh flowers mixes with the smell of home. Every house always has a distinctly different smell, and I never notice how much I love ours until I'm away for weeks on end every summer. It's always the most comforting feeling to smell it again. We spend the rest of the night filling our mom in on everything from Jason and Clara, to my newfound feelings for Henry, and Mr. Rolland's current situation that caused Henry to have to leave early. She expresses her excitement for Clara, just as shocked and proud as I was that Clara actually decided to give the boy a chance. She also encourages me with the right words, telling me it's never too late to fight for love, and that everything will work out *when* it's meant to *if* it's meant to, and I'm thankful for her words. She always knows the right things to say.

Later that night, I fall asleep the instant my head hits the pillow, and I dream of Henry and me reading in the Library Cafe, hands intertwined, August never-ending.

27

Chapter Twenty Seven

* * *

I wake up the next morning expecting to see mine and Clara's beach room when I open my eyes, but instead, I am met with my childhood bedroom before me. Turning over, I'm tempted to go back to sleep, but instead I decide to get up and start the day. I brush my teeth, change into some lounge-wear, and run downstairs to brew a fresh pot of coffee. The house is quiet. My mom sits on the couch reading a book while Clara remains asleep. It's just past eight once the coffee is done, and I pour myself a cup, adding some caramel oat milk creamer. I walk over to the front of the couch to give my mom a hug, needing it to start my day. Then, I head back upstairs and stand in the doorway of my room. It looks the same as it did when I was a teenager, threatening to pull me back to high school days. I imagine where I'd move things, pictures I'd put on the walls. I need a change of scenery if I am going to continue to live here while I figure out what the heck I'm doing with my life.

* * *

Sitting my coffee down on my desk, I begin to attempt to clear off and move my dresser, when my phone rings. I jump to grab it from my bed, and my heart leaps at the sight of Henry's name.

"Hey!" I answer as I set my phone up on my desk. Looking at the screen, I see he has his phone set up on something, too; the background behind him is an empty room. "Where are you?" I ask.

"*I* am in my *new* living room in my *new* apartment," he says as he reaches his arms out to his side as if to showcase it.

"Wow. A New York Apartment."

"Yeah," he says. "Check out this sick view."

He grabs the phone, and the image shakes as he moves it and flips the camera. When he does, the breathtaking skyline of the city that never sleeps shows up clear as day on the screen. I see the Empire State Building, and my heart fills equally with joy and sorrow. Joyful because this is a dream come true for Henry, and I'm so happy for him. Sorrowful because I realize I have let my hopes up with that last-minute internship opportunity, and I'd love nothing more than to be there chasing my dreams right now. Instead, I am rearranging my childhood bedroom, while Henry organizes his very first apartment in New York City. I hide any ounce of disappointment and focus on being happy for my best friend.

"That's a breathtaking view, Henry. I would never get used to it."

"Oh, I know. I can't wait to start my day with this view every morning," he says from behind the screen. The camera is still pointing towards the city's skyline. Even on camera, the sky looks so blue with perfectly shaped clouds floating alongside the tops of the skyscrapers. Henry turns the camera back around, and I catch the joy behind his eyes as he places his phone back up where he had it before.

"What are you up to today?"

"Oh, I'm just moving some furniture around. I need a change of scenery. What about you? When is your first day of your internship again?"

"Tomorrow morning. It's supposed to be a chill first day, from what I've heard, but I'm kind of nervous. I have to take the subway."

I laugh at the thought of Henry trying to navigate the subway, keeping to himself and standing near the door so he can be the first one off.

"Just get up early and you'll have plenty of time. From what I've heard, once you learn the subway system, it becomes second-nature. Are you going to miss your car?"

"Oh, I already do. But it is nice to be able to walk everywhere. The little neighborhood I live in is so cool. It's called the West Village. You'd love it here. There are coffee shops on every corner."

I smile at the thought of things there reminding him of me. *I think I would love it there.*

"Well, hopefully I can see it one day," I say. *I wish with all the hope in my heart as I say this aloud.*

Henry's smile in return is interrupted by an unknown number flashing on my screen. Confused, I walk over to pick my phone up off my desk where it has been sitting up. I usually ignore every unknown number, excusing it as spam. But, something in me tells me to pick it up before it goes to voicemail.

"Uh, hey Henry. I'm getting a random call, let me answer it and call you back, okay?"

"Sure. If I don't answer, it's because I'm out to brunch with my mom."

"Okay," is all I say for the sudden fear of this call leaving my screen. I hit the answer button and say hello at the same time that I hear the other line with Henry end.

"Hi! Is this Elena Martin?" A chipper lady's voice says on the other end.

I feel suddenly nervous, my stomach beginning to hurt a little.

"Yes, um, this is she."

"Hi, this is Jessica Sauntress with *The New Yorker.* I'm calling in regard to your creative and fiction writer internship application. I'm *so* sorry for the delay. It's been a train wreck over here trying to find someone to fill the position at such short notice. Our other candidate pulled out just last week, and we wanted to be thorough in choosing the next one to make sure it was someone who really wanted it. I noticed that in your application, you stated that your availability was immediate. Is that still the case?"

I'm not breathing. I don't think I've breathed a single breath since she said she was with *The New Yorker.* I force an inhale and exhale, and reply in a somewhat shaky voice.

"Yes. Yes. I am available immediately, of course."

I start to wonder if a one-worded *yes* would have sufficed, but she responds ecstatically.

"Great! We narrowed it down between you and one other applicant, but the other person said she would not be available for another two weeks. So, I wanted to check with you first since we're wanting someone here starting tomorrow."

"The internship starts tomorrow?"

"No! Sorry. The internship actually starts on Wednesday. However, we want our applicant to get settled starting tomorrow, on Monday. Since things are going to happen quickly, upon your acceptance of our offer, we will provide housing for you at an apartment of your choosing for up to two months while you get settled. We will also provide you with a plane ticket for any time tomorrow morning. We'd really like to have you on our team this year, Elena, so please let me know by the end of the day today, so that we can get all of the other details squared away."

"Yes," I say without even thinking.

"Oh! Are you positive you don't need any time to think it over?"

"Nope! I would be honored to accept this position!" I say, my heart beating faster and faster.

"Great! Well then, welcome to *The New Yorker*, Miss Elena Martin!"

I feel like I'm flying on cloud nine as she says this. *Welcome to The New Yorker.* I need someone to pinch me.

"We'll send you an email with flight information as well as apartments we're partnered with for you to select from. We would also like to get your permission to go ahead and publish your submission called *August's Promise.* It's a way for us to go ahead and get traction and feedback for you as an intern before you even start with us!"

I gulp, suddenly anxious at the thought of the most vulnerable thing I've ever written being available for everyone to see. Just as quickly as the anxiety comes, the excitement overshadows it. *I am about to be published in The New Yorker.* I am about to *work* at *The New Yorker.* If yesterday me could see myself now, she would have told me I was dreaming. If myself a *year ago* could see me now, she'd think this was a miracle. It *is* a miracle.

"Yes," I say again, seizing this opportunity that has fallen into my lap.

"Great!" Jessica says. "Well, I'll send over an email to you shortly, and I guess you should get to packing!"

I laugh, thankful that I didn't destroy my room trying to reorganize things.

"Yes! Thank you so much!"

"Thank you, Elena! I look forward to meeting you and working with you!"

"Me too!" I say.

We hang up, and I remain frozen in place, trying to let everything that just happened soak in. I don't think it will, until I'm there. In New

York City. With two days left of August, I start to think that maybe some promises were left unmet, so a bigger opportunity could come. I run into Clara's room while simultaneously yelling at our mom to come upstairs. I hear her footsteps rushing as I shake Clara awake. She groans as she sits up, pushing me away from her just as our mom reaches her doorway.

"What is it?" Our mom asks, panicked.

"Yeah. Why on earth are you disrupting me from my sleep? I had like thirty more minutes left until my alarm went off," Clara says while checking her phone on the nightstand.

"Okay. Are you guys ready?" I don't even know how to say it. They look at me with anticipation and impatience.

"I just got a last-minute acceptance as a creative and fiction writer intern with *The New Yorker*."

Silence. Shock. Jaws dropping.

"I leave tomorrow."

More silence falls between us, and then suddenly, I'm being engulfed in hugs on either side of me from my mom and my sister.

"Oh my gosh! What? How did this even happen? Ellie!" Clara hugs me tightly as she cheers in excitement.

My mom's arms tighten around me too as she says, "I can't believe you have to leave again already. But, I'm so so proud of you."

Tears threaten to fall, and I let them as I grab onto them. I'm thankful to be crying happy tears for once. After letting them go, we all pile onto Clara's bed, and I explain how this all came about. Clara asks me if I've told Henry, and I decide at that moment that I won't. I want to surprise him tomorrow. Maybe I can finally tell him everything I've been too scared to tell him. I won't wait for the "right" time anymore. I mean, if this isn't the right time… then when?

The three of us spend the rest of the day packing and checking and re-checking that I have everything I need. I pick an apartment complex in the West Village, trusting Henry's judgement and wanting to be close to him. Jessica emails me my flight information and apartment address, and I immediately order some furniture to be delivered there. I can't believe that just a few hours ago, I was looking at Henry's apartment view of the city through the phone, wishing that I could have the same one someday… and now, I have a new home in the city waiting for me. *Someday* turning into *tomorrow*.

* * *

The next morning was a rush to get to the airport in time, but now I'm here, and I feel all of the emotions as I check my bags and head towards security. I turn to my mom and Clara. Tears brim in both of their eyes, and mine. Tears that are full of happiness and sadness, but mostly happiness. I'll miss them, but I know they support me. They can see how much I want this, and I'm thankful to have a family that encourages me in the pursuit of my passions. I hug Clara tightly, and she doesn't object.

"I'm sorry, I won't be there to move you into your dorm. Send me pictures, okay?" She pulls away, keeping both of her hands over top of mine.

"It's okay. Jason's going to drive down to help. I'll FaceTime you, and *you* FaceTime me so I can see your apartment! I'm coming to visit on fall break, so make sure you make fun plans for us. I want to *live* like a New Yorker in the *fall*." She looks up as she says this, and I giggle, hugging her again.

"Sounds like a plan," I say.

I hug Mama next, and she tells me again just how proud she is of me. "Make a list of things you want me to make for dinner while you're home for Christmas, okay?"

"Oh, I will. Believe me," I say as I hug her tighter. Then, I see Nana and Papa jogging towards us from behind Mama as I'm hugging her still.

"Ellie girl!" Nana chimes, and Mama and I turn to welcome them to all the hugs and farewells.

"Oh, come here, you!" Nana brings me into a tight hug. "We are so proud of you."

I take in the familiar scent of her Coco Mademoiselle. "Thank you, Nana."

Papa is next, and it takes everything in me not to burst into tears. His eyes sparkle with pride and love as he brings me in for a squeeze.

"My best buddy, the city girl," he says, and I laugh against his chest.

As we pull apart, I take a second to fully take in the sight of my family before me. Their eyes all brimmed with tears and full of love, support, and belief in me. They have always believed in me, and I realize now that I've never truly been alone. And, with them in my life, I never would be. With one last group hug and words of encouragement, I head to the security line, looking back to wave at my sweet family one last time before turning the corner out of their sight. I walk towards my gate, and with each step I take, my heart beats faster in anticipation of the future that I'm getting closer to with each step.

* * *

When the plane lands, I'm thankful for how quickly I'm able to get off. I tried to rest my eyes for a while on the plane, but was too excited and nervous to really get any decent sleep. When I fully step into the airport, the terminal left behind me, I'm met with the hustle and bustle of traveling families and business people. I walk forward, following the signs to baggage claim, and pass an "I Heart New York" sign on the way. *I'm here. I'm actually in New York City.* I go to snap a picture, realizing I hadn't even turned my phone off of airplane mode yet. I was too eager to get off the plane.

Once my phone connects back to service, a multitude of texts come in. Most from my family, asking if I made it. I quickly text them back, and then freeze as I see about six texts from Henry. All of them are about his trek to the subway early this morning, and I laugh at the selfie he sent of himself, standing right next to the door, just as I thought he would. I see another text from Jules. She was overjoyed to hear about my news, and even more overjoyed to help me surprise Henry. Her text has the code to his apartment, which is going to be my first stop. She told me Henry's first day is only a half day, so I wanted to be at his apartment to surprise him when he gets home.

I look at the time. It's just after 9:30 a.m., so I have about two hours give or take until Henry might get back. With a deep breath, I go to claim my luggage and head out to hail a taxi. Just as I get outside, my phone starts to ring. A FaceTime call from Henry. I immediately hit decline, only for him to send a string of texts after. I ignore them too, as I see a yellow cab start to come into view.

Seizing the opportunity, I lift my hand to signal, and it pulls over to me almost instantly. *I feel like the main character of a movie right now.* As the taxi starts on its way into the city, I keep my eyes locked out the window, in anticipation of the world's most famous skyline to come into view. And when it does, I feel a surge of excitement in every inch of my being. *Hello, New York.*

* * *

"Here we are, Miss. The West Village." The taxi driver opens my door for me before proceeding to get my luggage out of the trunk. I turn in a slow circle, eyes lifted towards the sky as I take in the city before me. The buildings surrounding me are all connected, with different colored bricks forming beautiful homes. Beautifully designed staircases lead up to each door, and all of them are decorated with unique flowers and potted plants. I look to my right to see the apartment building we're in front of, and I can't believe my eyes. I feel like I'm in an episode of Friends as I make my way into the building, up the stairs, and to Henry's apartment door. I check the time again. It's just past 11:00 a.m. I type in the code, hands shaking, but before I even finish punching in the numbers, the door clicks, and my breath catches as I let out a gasp. It starts to swing open, and I hear an all too familiar voice.

"Mom, she's..." Henry stops talking as the door fully opens, revealing me on the other side of it.

"She's here," is all he says before he drops his phone to his side.

We're both frozen, eyes locked into one another's. His eyes are full of relief, joy, and what I hope... is *love*. I don't know where to begin as I stand frozen in the doorway of Henry's new apartment, our new lives about to start together as we stare in disbelief. Only another second goes by before Henry pulls me into him. His arms wrap around me, and he lifts me off the ground slightly, pulling me into the apartment fully. I keep my arms wrapped tightly around his neck, wanting to be as close to him as possible, constantly wrapped in his arms so that I know this isn't a dream.

After what feels like forever, I'm met with a chill in the air as he pulls back, the warmth of his hug escaping me. He blinks a few times, as if he can't believe his eyes either.

"How?"

"Let's sit down," I say. He motions me over to a blow-up air mattress in the middle of the empty living room.

"Sorry, this is all I have for the next couple of days."

I laugh and plop down as he wheels my luggage into the apartment, shutting the door behind him. His eyes are full of wonder, and I feel suddenly shy as he takes a seat next to me on the air mattress, shifting me slightly up higher at the impact. He looks over to me, and I can almost feel his breath. I notice the space behind him on the mattress and take note of how he chose to sit as close to me as possible.

"I got a last-minute spot as an intern at *The New Yorker,*" I blurt out.

Shock fills his bright eyes, the sun from the vast window behind us reflecting pools of honey in them. I finally take in his suit and tie at the close proximity. *The city looks good on him.*

"Wait, what? Are you kidding?"

I shake my head, and he beams with happiness as he pulls me in for yet another hug.

"That's amazing, El." His voice is a whisper as he rubs his hand down my hair. I take a deep breath, feeling at home in his arms. We pull apart too soon, and his eyes search mine for more.

"I start on Wednesday," I say.

He blinks in disbelief yet again. "Wait. What? How in the world? Where are you going to live? That's so fast!

"Well, I was thinking… the West Village?"

His smile beams brighter, and it's my favorite sight I've ever seen. More than the New York City skyline.

"This is insane, El. Insane and amazing! So… you're here to *stay* then, huh?"

There's emphasis on the word *stay* as he asks for confirmation.

"I'm here to stay," I say. And that familiar look of love and longing flickers behind his golden eyes again.

"I have to show you something," I say, and he nods, brows furrowing at my sudden change of topic. I move to grab my laptop from my carry-on bag, opening it up to the final edited version of my piece on love that I had approved for publication in *The New Yorker.*

I take a deep breath as I hold my laptop out to Henry, choosing not to sit back down next to him. He takes it into his hands and glances at the screen for half a second before I interrupt.

"This is essentially what got me here. I want you to read it. But, I don't want to stand here while you do… so can I freshen up in your bathroom for a few minutes?"

He nods with a full grin, and I feel my cheeks already heating up as he looks back down at my laptop in concentration. I jog into the bathroom, locking the door behind me. I take a deep breath and lean against the sink counter. When I come back out of this bathroom, Henry Rolland will know, without a doubt… that *I am in love with him.*

28

Chapter Twenty Eight

* * *

Henry

I watch as Elena shuts the door to the bathroom behind her, still not believing the sight before my eyes. *She's here. She's really here, and she's staying.* I shake my head in disbelief and turn my attention to her laptop in front of me. The title *August's Promise* is at the top of the screen, and I smile to myself, expecting a beautiful picture of summers spent at Orange Beach. I don't wait another second as I begin to read, having missed the way she orchestrates words so beautifully.

August's Promise

Promises of August come like the wind. Full of force, sweeping me off my feet, then gone too soon. Every summer, I wait for August to uphold its promises. To mute reality and bring me into its warmth and love.

Love.

That is the promise. Every year I wait. Every year I yearn... to escape the loneliness. To escape the troubles of the rest of the world. To feel my problems float away in the waves of the ever-flowing sea. It works every time. The waves crashing to the shore, casting out the noise in my mind.

Peace.

Traditions.

Time under the sun.

Wading in the water.

An escape from reality is all I ever needed.

The promises of August.

Or, so I thought.

I thought this place would always be my great escape. This month would never disappoint me. Not here. Not by the sea. How could it?

But it did.

August has broken promise after promise.

Rainfall.

Interruptions.

Noise.

Self-doubt.

Thoughts creeping in, drowning out the sound of the peaceful waves that used to overshadow it. August, what are you doing? Why break the promises when I need them most? When I've yearned for them the most? Hope lost. I'm overwhelmed. I don't know what to think. What to do.

Until... you.

You bring me peace when the sounds of waves breaking fail to.

You bring me comfort when another promise has been broken, traditions interrupted.

You silence my thoughts with just the sound of your voice when I can't seem to escape them.

You bring me back down to the ground, reminding me that I am safe with just one look in your warm eyes.

Your laughter replaces all the other noise.

My favorite sound.

You are my favorite promise of August.

I count down the days to get to you.

My favorite reality is the one with you in it.

I want it every August.

I want it every day, of every month, of every year.

You.

You are the one who taught me that a simple month is not the source of every promise made.

Every promise kept.

It's not August, I wish to escape to each year.

It's you.

August doesn't keep the promises.

Nor does the ocean's vastness as it welcomes me each summer, always the same. Never moving.

Wave after wave.

Promise after promise.

August after August.

You.

You are the promise that I want forever.

A promise of love.

Of friendship.

Of support and hope in every season.

Seasons where reality is heavy, like waves crashing violently on the shore.

Seasons where reality seems to flow like a calm sea.

Coasting together.

Laughing together.

Keeping promises together

The promise of love.
That is August's Promise.
The Promise that I want to keep and hold onto with you.
Forever.

I re-read her words for a second time, my pulse quickening as I take in the picture she's painted.

The picture she's painted of me. For me.

The bathroom door creaks open, and I close her laptop as she pads over to me slowly. Her cheeks are red, and I can feel that mine are too. I stand up, and as I do, she stops abruptly in place, no longer walking towards me. Her hands are held together behind her back, and she looks up at me with a shy look behind her beautiful blue eyes.

My El.

All summer, I counted down the days I had left with her. Every moment she spent with Kyle felt like torture. When I saw how much I'd hurt her by not being able to muster up the courage to write to her... I felt the shame and guilt in my whole being.

The day we said yes to everything all day. That was *the* day. The day that it all clicked for me, that I was an idiot for not realizing what's been right in front of me all along. She floated before me in the water that day, her laughter bringing her smile to her eyes after we'd jumped off the rock together, hand in hand, facing fears. I realized then that I'd jump hand in hand with her over any hurdle in life. Off any cliff. I'd go to any destination, as long as she was by my side.

I remember feeling like my time was running out. I remember the feeling of my hands around her waist, taking every ounce of self-control I had to not kiss her in that moment as I felt her skin under the water. But now, here in this empty New York apartment, as she stands in front of me with that look of love and want in her eyes, every ounce of my self-control goes out the window. I take a giant step towards her, placing one hand lightly around the back of her neck, the other falling to her waist, gripping as her lips... *finally* crash into mine.

29

Chapter Twenty Nine

* * *

Henry's lips on mine feel like the perfect puzzle piece, finally finding its place after searching for it forever. His lips part and move in sync with mine as if we've done this forever. *I want to do this forever.*

I bring my hands to the back of his neck, turning my head every so slightly to feel more of him. He makes a sound of pleasure as I bring my body closer to him, his hands tightening around either side of my waist. Our breath quickens together with every movement of our lips, and I sigh into him as we take our time, savoring every kiss, every brush of skin, every breath we take together. Just as things start to heat up more, he takes a step back, his eyes wild.

"I've wanted to do that for a while now," he says, catching his breath and tucking a strand of hair behind my ear. His other hand doesn't move from my waist. *I never want it to.*

"Me too," I say as a blush creeps onto my face.

Henry grins the deepest grin I've ever seen.

"My, El," he says, his thumb rubbing my cheek.

My stomach flips, and my heart melts as he says this.

"Your writing… El. When did you… I mean, how long have you…"

"I think… I've always loved you. It just took its time revealing itself to me. But when it did, it came all at once. Full force. My love for you is not to be ignored, Henry Rolland."

He laughs. "Good, I don't want you to ignore it." He rubs my cheek with his thumb again and takes a deep breath before saying, "Because I love you too, Elena Martin."

Tears well up in my eyes, but before they has a chance to fall, his lips crash into mine again, the rest of the world falling silent as we both escape into this new reality, and new promises are brewing as we welcome them with open arms.

I wake up later to the smell of freshly popped popcorn coming from Henry's kitchen. Rolling over on the now slightly deflated air mattress, I look out the floor-to-ceiling window that's cascaded with golden hues as the endless buildings reflect the golden hour from nearly every direction. It makes his empty living room seem so cozy, and as I continue to look at the empty space, I start to easily imagine where he'd put his furniture. I start to easily imagine coming over to have dinner with him after our busy days at our internships. I'd give his shoulders a massage while he plays with my hair as we unwind together at the end of every day.

The image is as warm as the hue that continues to shine through, the rays shifting ever so slightly as clouds move in front of the sun. They move perfectly to where Henry now stands in the kitchen, having changed into sweatpants and a hoodie. He's pulling the now steaming bag of popcorn out of the microwave. I watch him silently as he then grabs a large bowl, pouring it all in. When he finally looks up, his smile that breaks is my favorite sight to see, and now I can see it whenever I want.

"Good morning," he says sarcastically as he grabs the bowl and walks back over to where I still lie comfortably on the half-inflated air mattress.

"You don't have any furniture, yet you somehow managed to make sure to stock up on popcorn," I say with a laugh. Not surprised.

"Always," he says as he plops down next to me.

I adjust the blanket, welcoming him into the warmth. As I dig my hand into the bowl of popcorn, I start to wish we had M&Ms. Before I even mention this, I watch as he grabs his backpack that sits in the corner of the room and pulls out his laptop and a bag of M&Ms.

"No way," I say in disbelief.

He laughs and gets situated back in the makeshift bed we've made. "I planned on calling you tonight so we could watch a movie together over the phone or something. But, this is even better."

"It's perfect," I say.

The sun is lower now, the golden hour slightly reflecting in his deep brown eyes now. I don't care how long I'm staring into them this time. I want to get lost in them forever. I swear they glisten brighter, and I find more flecks of golden honey the more his gaze pours into mine. A grin tugs at his mouth before he places his hand around the back of my neck, pulling me into a kiss again. I will never get used to kissing him. I break a smile into the kiss, earning a subtle laugh from him. He pulls back slightly, his hand now caressing my cheek as his eyes pour into me still.

"What's got you smiling, El?"

"You."

His own smile grows as he pulls me into a kiss again, the popcorn bowl between us knocking over, but we both don't seem to care. All we care about is this moment, right here. And, the fact that we get to keep having moments like this even after August ends, as new promises await us both. Together.

Epilogue

* * *

One Year Later

I don't realize I had fallen asleep until the abrupt halt of the subway, followed by the robotic voice calling out my stop, jolts me awake. Today I had to review about a dozen manuscripts to meet my goal before I catch a flight in the morning to head down to Alabama. Henry and I are both receiving a little vacation time after accepting full-time positions that came from our internships. We both extended our leases on our West Village apartments for at least another six months as soon as our new positions became official, and it still doesn't feel real. We get to continue to pursue our passions alongside each other in one of the world's most exciting cities, that has become our new home.

Henry was able to get off a couple of days earlier than I, so he used the time to visit with Jules and his dad before heading down to our little slice of paradise. *Orange Beach.* He'll greet me there with the rest of the family tomorrow, and I can't wait. I love this city, but I do miss the ocean. Henry and I have been living just down the hall from each other, and it's felt like a dream. I get to pop over every morning I want, cooking us breakfast on the weekends, and having lazy Sundays together. We've watched movie after movie, had writing sessions after writing sessions at our favorite neighborhood coffee shop called Partners. It's no Library Cafe, but it's a New York coffee shop, so you can't really go wrong there.

He's taken me out on fun dates as we've used them as excuses to get out and explore the city. He took me to the top of the Empire State Building and kissed me there on New Year's Eve just as the ball dropped. It was the most romantic main character movie moment of my life. My Nana was right. Dating your best friend is the way to go. *Loving* your best friend is such a gift.

The memories and moments of this past year are replaying in my head, and I'm sure that I'm smiling to myself like a crazy person as I shuffle with the crowd of commuters out of the subway doors, climbing the steps to come out on Charles St. As I emerge from the chaos of the subway below, I look around my little neighborhood, taking it in once again. I still can't believe this is my life… and it gets to keep being my life. But not during August. August belongs to the sea.

* * *

The next morning, I board my flight and text our family group chat, which includes both the Rollands and the Martins, before turning my phone on airplane mode and diving into my own book. The book I've been writing. It's about a place that's brought me love and peace, and the people that mean the most to me. The place I'm finally getting to go to again, knowing promises won't be broken… because Henry will be there and our love is a promise like no other.

As soon as the Uber drops me off in front of the familiar blue and white houses, I can feel my heart swelling. Clara runs out the front door, nearly tackling me. After spending so much time apart, hugs have become a much more normal occurrence for us both. She looks absolutely stunning, college becoming her. I hug her tightly, watching as Jason smiles at us, waving from the porch. We pull apart, and Clara has tears brimming in her eyes, her smile wider than I've ever seen it before. She takes my luggage from my hands, and I go to protest, but she stops me.

"No, no. I've got this. You need to go see Henry at his house."

"What? Why? Is everything okay?"

Clara says nothing, but just walks away with a poor excuse for a wink of the eye. I watch as Jason takes my luggage from her, his smile also wider than I've ever seen it before too. Confused, I slowly make my way up the stairs to Henry's blue house, my heartbeat quickening the closer I get.

Opening the door, the house is dark. No sight of Henry or even Jules anywhere. I see a dim light coming from up the stairs, and I laugh as I hear Henry's song playing from the Alexa speaker in the kitchen. It's not him singing, but it's *his words* about *his love* for *me*. His first song he sold from his internship, and my favorite song in the world. When I get to the bottom of the stairs, starting my way up, my eyes begin to brim with tears as I notice the rose petals of all colors resting upon each step of the stairs I take. When I get to the door of his loft room, I take a deep breath, attempting to compose myself, before lightly pushing the door open.

When I do, my breath is taken away as the room before me is lit with candles everywhere, the rose petals placed in a perfect circle on the floor, and Henry standing there in the middle, dressed in the black button-up shirt I got him for Christmas, his face clean-shaven just the way I like it. His hair is styled slightly, but one piece has escaped and falls on his forehead… and I *love* it. He has one hand remaining behind his back as he uses the other to reach out to me, and my hand shakes as I place it into his. Leading me to stand in the circle of rose petals, I let out a choked cry that is coated with a nervous laugh before he even says a word, and he begins to laugh too, tears filling his eyes.

"Good to see you," he says with the purest look of adoration in his eyes. His hand squeezes mine as I laugh again, and I rub my thumb over his hand in return.

"You too," I laugh.

He sighs, and then he does the very thing I had been anticipating since I saw the first rose petal coming up the stairs just seconds ago. Since we first kissed in that empty New York apartment a year ago. Since I realized I've loved him for longer than I ever knew. Henry Rolland gets down on one knee before me, a ring showcased in his hand as he pops open the box he had held behind his back. I instinctively bring a hand over my mouth, my breathing short and quick now.

"Elena Martin. My best friend. The love of my life. I think, no matter what, we would have ended up in this position right here, my knee knelt before you as I ask you to be my wife. You are the best thing that has ever happened to me, and I feel so lucky that our story started here, in these houses, on this beach. This is where I want the rest of our lives to truly start together. I want to promise my love to you forever in the place where this promise was made long before we both even realized it."

Tears are pouring down both of our cheeks now.

"I want to learn with you forever, grow with you forever, experience this love with you forever, and I want this promise to begin, yet again as we both say *I do.* There is no one else I want to make this promise with but you, Elena Martin. A promise to love you for the rest of my life, if you will do me the honors... of marrying me?"

I don't even have to think as I reach down and motion for him to stand up, uttering *yes, yes, yes* as I crash my lips into his.

He instantly lifts me off the ground, spinning me in a circle, and I giggle in pure joy. He sets me down, taking my hand to place the most perfect diamond ring on my finger. It has a silver band and a cluster of three diamonds, two dainty ones that sit on either side of an oval-cut one. It's simple, and it's perfect… because it's from my best friend. The love of my life, and as he slips it on my finger, it represents the best promise of the rest of our lives.

* * *

After spending a few more moments alone together, barely being able to keep our hands off each other, Henry takes my hand and leads me back over to my house. When we walk in, Henry holds my left hand in the air, the ring reflecting the light that comes pouring in from the windows that let in the sun's rays. I instantly cry tears of joy at the sight before me. Cheers and claps from my family. Nana and Papa stand in one corner, Papa's eyes glossy and Nana's smile wide as ever. Clara and Jason stand cheering with arms around each other, and next to her are my mom and dad, clapping next to Jules and James. James has a look of pure joy in his eyes, and I feel happy that he's finally happy for his son, and all that he's accomplished, and now… the life we're about to start together.

Henry kisses my cheek, and we begin to make our rounds of greeting everyone, and I've never felt a joy as pure as this.

As everyone begins to dig into Nana's famous chocolate cake, I take a second to myself, stepping out onto the back porch. With one inhale of the salty ocean air, I slip out of my shoes and go to greet the ocean. My feet sink deeper and deeper into the sand with each wave that makes its way to shore.

"Thank you, August," I whisper out into the vast blue ocean before me.

An arm wraps around me, and I know it's my husband to be without even looking. I lean into him as he shifts to place both arms around my waist, his head resting on top of mine.

"Ready to keep the longest promise of your life?" He asks jokingly, but I answer in the most sure and steady voice as I turn to face him, his hands clasped together as they fall to my lower back and rest there.

"I've been ready for this promise forever," I say, and he looks at me with love in his eyes that has become the look he gives me the most, always so telling and pure. He pulls me in for a kiss, and I sigh into it as the peaceful sound of the ocean enters with us into the new reality of the rest of our lives together… the best promise August will ever bring.

Afterword

I want to thank every single person who picked up this book and gave it a chance. I have loved reading for my entire life. I have loved writing for my entire life. Written words really do just bring about whole new worlds to escape to, and I hope that you enjoyed escaping to this one with these characters.

This book had moments that were inspired by my sister's and my annual trips to Orange Beach, Alabama, with our Nana and Papa every summer. I want to note that the brief personalities and stories of Nana and Papa in this novel were about 90% based on truth. My grandparents met in high school in the 60s, and I loved that I was able to highlight some of their story within this one.

I also would like to note that the chapter in which Papa and Elena came across a Bull Shark was based on a true event that happened to my Papa and me one summer at Orange Beach! It played out essentially the same, except I was much younger and definitely not as calm. Clara was inspired by my little sister Caroline, and she is my best friend in the whole world.

If you enjoyed this book, I hope that you will follow me @emilyjoycewrites on Instagram and Substack. I desire to be a full-time author one day, and this is just the beginning. It would help me, and mean so much if you gave a Goodreads review and told your friends about my book! I can't wait to continue this journey. It's been such a blessing to be able to write my first novel and share it with the world.

Thank you again, so much to my family and loved ones. Those who heard me talk about my days spent writing at endless coffee shops. Those who encouraged me and walked alongside me as I pursued this passion. You all know exactly who you are. Thank you for your support. And, last but certainly not least, thank you, Kavi Collins, for creating the beautiful and most perfect cover and design for my entire book! I could not have done this without you.

Until the next writing journey, thank you again. All glory to the Lord.

-Emily Joyce

www.ingramcontent.com/pod-product-compliance
Lightning Source LLC
Chambersburg PA
CBHW032257310726

48973CB00008B/2437